D1500319

TÁRÁBAS

A GUEST ON EARTH

TÁRÁBÁS

A GUEST ON EÁRTH

BY

JOSEPH ROTH

THE OVERLOOK PRESS

Woodstock • New York

First published in 1987 by
The Overlook Press
Lewis Hollow Road
Woodstock, New York 12498

Library of Congress Cataloging-in-Publication Data

Roth, Joseph, 1894-1939.
  Tarabas, a guest on earth.

  I. Title.
PT2635.084T28 1987 833'.912 86-31239
ISBN 0-87951-275-X

Printed in the U.S.A.

CONTENTS

PART ONE

THE TRIAL

1

IN August of the year nineteen-hundred-and-fourteen there lived in New York a young man named Nicholas Tarabas. By nationality he was Russian. He belonged to one of those races, which at that time the great Tsar ruled over, and which are known today as the "western border-nations."

Tarabas was the son of well-to-do parents. He had studied at the technical college in St. Petersburg. Less actual conviction than the unfocused ardour of his young heart had led him, during his third term as a student, to join a revolutionary society which was shortly afterwards implicated in a bombing outrage against the governor of Kherson. Tarabas and his comrades were brought to trial. Some were convicted, others acquitted. Among the latter was Tarabas. His father turned him out of doors and promised him money if he would agree to emigrate to America. Young Tarabas left his native land as unthinkingly as he had become a revolutionary two years before. He followed his curiosity and the call of the far unknown, carefree and strong, and filled with confidence in a "new life."

Only he had not been two months in the great stone
city when homesickness woke in him. The world still
lay before him, and yet it sometimes seemed as though
it already lay far behind. There were days when he
felt like an old man, filled with longing for his wasted
life and with the knowledge that he has no time left
to start another one. And so he let himself drift, as the
phrase is, and made no attempt to adapt himself to his
new surroundings nor to look about for a means of
livelihood. He yearned for the soft blue haze on the
fields of his childhood, for the frozen furrows in winter, the larks' keen trilling all the summer long, the
fragrance of potatoes roasting in autumn fields, the
croaking songs of frogs down in the swamps, and
the edged whisper of crickets in the meadows. Nicholas
bore nostalgia in his heart. He hated New York, the
tall buildings, the wide streets, and all else that was
stone. And New York was a city of stone.

A month or two after his arrival he had made the
acquaintance of Katharina, a girl from Nizhny-
Novgorod. She was a waitress. Tarabas loved her like
his lost home. He could talk to her; he might love her,
taste her, smell her. She reminded him of his father's
fields, of the Russian sky, of the fragrance of roasting
potatoes in the autumn ploughland of his childhood.
Katharina was not from his district. But she spoke the
language he could understand. And she understood
his moods and did not thwart them. The songs she

sang he too had learnt at home, and she knew people of the same kind as he had known.

He was jealous, wild, and tender, as ready with kisses as with blows. For hours together he would loiter in the café where Katharina was employed. He would often sit long at one of her tables, watching her, the men waiters, and the customers, and sometimes he would go into the kitchen to observe the cook as well. The presence of Nicholas Tarabas began to make others feel uncomfortable. The owner of the café threatened to dismiss Katharina. Tarabas threatened to kill the owner of the café. Katharina asked her friend to come there no more. But jealousy drove him back again and again. One evening he committed an act of violence which was to alter the course of his life. But first this happened:

On a sultry day in late summer he went out to Coney Island, New York's great amusement park. He wandered aimlessly from one booth to another. He flung meaningless wooden balls at worthless china objects; with gun, pistol, and antiquated bow and arrow he shot at foolish figures and set them in foolish motion; he bestrode horses, donkeys, camels, and let them revolve with him on merry-go-rounds; seated in a boat he traversed grottoes full of mechanical ghosts and sinister gurgling waters; he enjoyed the shocks of violent soaring and descent upon the scenic-railway, and in the chamber of horrors he looked at the anomalies of nature, venereal disease, and notorious murderers. At last he stopped outside a booth where a gipsy engaged to tell the fate of those who would show her their hands. Tarabas was superstitious. He had already taken many an opportunity to cast a glance into the future; he had consulted the interpreters of stars and cards, and had himself delved into all manner of literature dealing with astrology, hypnosis, and suggestion. White horses and chimney-sweeps, nuns, monks, and priests, met in the street, determined where he should go, the roads he should take, the direction of his walks and his most trivial decisions. He was careful to avoid old women and red-haired people in the morning. And Jews who chanced to cross his path on Sundays he looked upon as certain harbingers of evil. These matters largely occupied his waking hours.

Before the gipsy's tent, therefore, he stopped. The upturned barrel, in front of which she sat upon a stool, was spread with the paraphernalia of her sorcery—a glass ball filled with some green fluid, a yellow wax candle, playing cards and a small pile of silver coins, a little rod of rusty-brown wood, and stars of shining gold-leaf, large and small. There was a crowd before the fortune-teller's booth, but no one had yet dared to go up to her. She was young, handsome, and indifferent. She did not seem even to see the people. She kept her brown, beringed hands folded in her lap, and her eyes downcast and fixed upon them. Her garish red silk blouse did not hide the living breath of her full bosom. Great gold coins quivered along the heavy chain wound three times round her neck. She wore similar coins in her ears. And it was as if a clink and clangor went out from all that metal, although in reality one heard no sound from it. The gipsy did not seem at all concerned to be the paid intermediary between the supernatural powers and the creatures of earth, but seemed rather to be one of those powers themselves, which do not reveal to men their destiny but ordain it.

Tarabas pushed his way through the crowd, approached the barrel, and offered his hand without a word. Slowly the gipsy raised her eyes. She looked Tarabas in the face until, his self-assurance wavering, he made a movement as though to withdraw. He felt the warmth of the brown fingers and the coolness of the silver rings upon his outspread hand. Little by little, very gently, his elbows brushing the glass ball as he stooped, the woman drew him over towards her till his face was close to hers. The people behind him pressed nearer; he felt their curiosity. That, their curiosity, seemed to be what was forcing him over towards the fortune-teller, and he would have liked to step across the tub to rid himself of them, and be alone with her. He was afraid lest she might talk about him too loudly and that they would hear—and he was about to change his mind and go away again.

"Don't be afraid," she said in the language of his own country, "nobody will understand me. But first give me two dollars, and take care the others see you. Many of them will go away then."

It startled him that she had guessed his mother-tongue. She took the money with her left hand, held it up a while for the people to see, and put it down upon the tub. Then she spoke in Tarabas's own language. "You are very unlucky, sir. I read in your hand that you are a murderer and a saint. There is no unhappier fate in all the world. You will sin and atone—and both upon this earth."

The gipsy released Tarabas's hand. She dropped her eyes, clasped her hands in her lap, and was motionless again. Tarabas turned to go. The people made way for him, full of respect for a man who had given two dollars to a gipsy. The fortune-teller's words stood separate in his memory, without coherence; he could repeat them as they had been said to him. He wandered without interest among the shooting-booths and marvels, turned back, resolved to desert the park, thought about Katharina, whom he would soon be going to fetch as usual, remembered that he had felt her growing distant towards him lately, and tried to fight the feeling down. It was the end of August. . . .

The sky was grey and leaden, a narrow sky in narrow streets, between high stone buildings. One told oneself that a storm would come. It did not. This country was ruled by other laws; nature allowed the practical mankind of this country to say what she should do and not do. They, for the moment, did not need a storm. Tarabas left the park. He rode down to the café, to Katharina. So he was a murderer and a saint. He had been set apart for great things.

The nearer he came to Katharina's café, the clearer grew, so he believed, the meaning of the prophecy. The gipsy's words began to string themselves together on a cord of sense. So, thought Tarabas, I am first to be a murderer and then a saint. (Fate, spinning her threads without regard to Tarabas, could not be met, as it were, half-way by means of changing the course of life from that moment on by an act of will—this was not possible.)

Tarabas, entering the café, was disturbed at missing Katharina from among the waitresses, and at receiving, upon asking where she was, the answer that she had asked for a day off, which had been given her. She should, however, be back again by nine o'clock, they said. Therein he saw the first beginning of the fate which had been foretold him. He sat down at a table and ordered a gin of the waitress who knew him well as Katharina's friend; and he concealed his unrest behind one of those witticisms which waiters everywhere are accustomed to receive from old habitués. But as he found the time very long, he followed the first order with another, and a third. And as he was a poor

drinker, he soon began to lose his sane grasp of the
things of this world, and of the circumstances and
occasion, and began superfluously to make a great deal
of noise.

Hereupon the owner, a powerful, well-nourished
fellow with whom Tarabas had been out of favour for
a long time, came over and requested him to leave the
café. Tarabas swore, paid, left the café, but, to the
other's chagrin, remained standing at the entrance to
wait for Katharina. A few minutes later she came, her
face flushed, her hair dishevelled, clearly in extreme
haste, fear in her eyes, and, to Tarabas, prettier than
he had ever seen her.

"Where have you been?" he asked.

"At the post-office," said Katharina. "There was a
registered letter, I had to go and fetch it; I wasn't here
when the postman came. My father's ill; he's going to
die maybe. I must go back home. As soon as I can. Can
you help me? Have you got any money?"

Jealous and mistrustful, Tarabas searched the eyes,
the voice, the face of his beloved, to find a lie and a
deception lurking somewhere. He looked at her with
penetrating and reproachful sadness for a long while,
and she, now utterly confused, bent her head. Then—
and already rage was seething in him—he said:

"A lie—I thought so. Well, where were you?"

At the same instant he remembered that today was
Wednesday, and the cook would be free as well. This

was a reality, a living figure for his suspicion to seize upon. Terrible pictures rolled with the speed of lightning across his mind. His fists clenched, he pushed Katharina in the side. She staggered, losing her hat; her hand-bag fell to the ground. Tarabas snatched it up and rummaged in it wildly, asking over and over again what she had done with her father's letter. It was not to be found.

"I must have lost it. I was so upset," Katharina stammered, and big tears stood in her eyes.

"Lost it, eh?" roared Tarabas.

A few passers-by had noticed them and stopped. Now the owner of the café came out. He put his left arm round Katharina for protection and pushed her behind him; he thrust his right arm towards Tarabas and cried:

"No rows outside my place! You clear out! And don't let me see you around here any more!"

Tarabas raised his fist and drove it full into the man's face. A tiny drop of blood appeared upon the wide bridge of the nose, ran down the cheek, became a thin red stripe. "Good hit," thought Tarabas; his heart rejoiced; his fury was still rising. The blood that he had shed kindled desire to see more. It was the moment when his blood began to flow that seemed to make the owner of the café Tarabas's real, great enemy, the only one he had in all New York, that mighty place of stone. When now the enemy put his hand into his

pocket to look for a handkerchief to wipe away the
blood, Tarabas believed that he was feeling for his
gun. Therefore he hurled himself upon him; like
talons his fingers bit deep into the neck and choked
until the café-owner came down with his head striking
the glass door of the bar. A monstrous din filled Tarabas's brain. The splintering crash of the glass, the dull
impact of the enemy's body, the simultaneous cry of
gaping onlookers, at once frightened and amused, of
the waitresses and customers from the café, all flowed
together into a sea of fearful sound. Together with his
man, his hands on the powerful throat, Tarabas too
had fallen to the ground. He felt the muscular, taut
belly through the coat and vest; the enemy's staring
mouth showed the red maw, the pale grey gums with
the tongue moving between them like some strange
beast, the flashing white of the strong teeth. Tarabas
saw the bubbles of froth at the corners of the mouth,
the bluely tarnished lips, the jerked-up chin.

All at once an unknown grip had Tarabas by the
scruff of his neck; it closed on him, strangled him,
lifted him up. The pain and the force of it were too
much. His own grip slackened. He looked round no
more. He neither looked nor saw another thing. Suddenly fear had caught him. With strong shoves he
parted the crowd, tumult still in his ears, immense
vague terror in his breast. With great leaps he bounded
across the street, pursuers and shouts and the shrill

whistle of a policeman in his wake. He ran. He felt
himself running. He ran as though he had six pairs of
legs, magnificent power in thighs and feet, freedom
before his eyes, death at his back. He ran into a side
street, and threw a glance behind. No sign of his
hunters. He fled into a dark doorway, cowered behind
the staircase, saw and heard the pursuing horde speed
past the house. People were coming downstairs. He
held his breath. An eternity, it seemed to him, he
crouched there in silence.

It might have been inside a grave. It was a coffin he
was crouched in. Somewhere an infant wailed. Children were shouting in the yard. These voices reassured
Tarabas. He pulled his shirt, his suit, his tie, to rights.
He got up and went warily to the outside door. The
street wore an ordinary look. Tarabas left the house.
Evening had come. Already the street-lamps were
alight, and the shop windows shone out up and down
the road.

2

SOON, to his consternation, Tarabas discovered himself returning to the café. He faced about, turned a corner into a side street, where he lost his bearings, argued that he must keep to the left, only to realize a few seconds later that he had described a right-angle and had come out near the restaurant again. Meanwhile, according to his wont, he had kept a look-out for some sign of good or evil omen, a white horse, a nun, a red-haired person, a red-haired Jew, an old woman, a hunchback. No sign forthcoming, he decided to endow other things with fateful import. He began to count lamp-posts and paving-stones, the little square holes in the gratings underfoot, the shut and open windows of this house and that, and the number of his own steps from a set point on the sidewalk to the next crossing. Thus busy testing oracles of every kind, he came on one of those early moving-picture theatres, long, narrow, and mercifully dark, which in those days were still called bioscopes, and sometimes kept their variegated programmes turning the whole night through until daybreak without interruption. As it now seemed to Tarabas that this theatre had suddenly appeared before him—as opposed to his having approached it consciously—he took this for a sign, bought a ticket, and entered the unlighted hall, escorted by the usher's yellow lamp.

He took his seat—not, as he usually did, on the aisle, but in the middle of the row amongst the other people, and close to the screen, though from that point he could not see the picture properly. He was resolved to give his whole attention to what was going on before him. For a while he could not succeed in doing so, either because he had come in in the middle of the story, or because he was too near. He had to crane his neck to see, the row in which he sat being too far below the level of the screen, and soon it became painful. But gradually the story captured him, and he tried to guess the beginning of it, as though it were one of those puzzles in the illustrated papers, the solution of which often beguiled his hours of waiting for Katharina.

It was now clear to him that the story on the screen was concerned with the fate of a curious man who, guiltless, and indeed from noble motives—to protect a woman, in fact—had become a criminal, a murderer, thief, and burglar, and who, misunderstood by the lady in distress for whose sake he had performed so many gruesome deeds, was put in prison, into a horrible cell, condemned to death, and finally conducted to the gallows. Asked, according to custom, to express a last wish, he begged for leave to write the name of his beloved in his own blood upon the wall of his cell, and for the promise of the authorities that it should never be effaced. With a knife lent him by the executioner's assistant he made an incision in his left hand, dipped the first finger of the right into the blood, and wrote upon the stone wall of the cell the sweetest name of all—"Evelyn." These proceedings took place, as one could see by the costumes, not in America, nor yet in England, but in one of the legendary Balkan countries of the Continent. The hero died imperturbably upon the scaffold.

The screen was quiet and empty. The pleasant hum of the cinema apparatus ceased, as did the piano which accompanied the dramas. For a few moments Tarabas was left to wonder whether, in the play he had just seen, he should recognize an allusion to his own experience plain enough to warrant his taking it to be the sign which he believed heaven always sent him for his guidance.

There was certainly a resemblance between the hero and himself, and between Evelyn and Katharina. Before, however, he had had time to decide the matter definitely, the screen lit up again and a new film began.

This time the theme was biblical, namely the shearing of Samson by Delilah, in order to make him weak and subservient to the Philistines. If, under the influence of the foregoing piece, Tarabas had felt disposed to surrender himself to earthly justice and suffer the

heroic fate which had seemed to bring him near to the
man on the gallows, now the figure of Samson, meting
out vengeance on Delilah and the Philistines, though
blind, inspired him with a preference for that still
more imposing end. And, contriving a resemblance
now between Katharina and Delilah, he began to con-
fuse them with each other. He wondered, in view of
the extreme dissimilarity between American and biblical conditions, how he should manage to effect his
vengeance on the world of Philistines in the manner of
the Judean hero. Miracles must take place in New
York no less than in the ancient land of Israel. And
with the help of God, who was probably not ill disposed towards Tarabas either, one could pull down
the mighty pillars of the law-courts and the prison.
Tarabas felt strength in every muscle. He was still in
his heart a firm believer. It was a long time now since
he had been to church. As a young man and a student,
dedicated to the revolutionary ideal, he had given notice to the God his childhood had held in awe that he
neither believed in Him nor would obey Him any
longer; and soon afterwards he had fallen a prey to his
belief in chimney-sweeps, white horses, and red-headed
Jews. These notwithstanding, he still loved and cherished the conception of a God Who never forsook the
believer, and Who held all sinners dear. That was true;
God loved him, Nicholas Tarabas. His mind was made
up; when the programme was over, he would give

himself up to earthly justice, piously confident of the clemency of heaven.

But weariness overcame him—and moreover the programme began again from the beginning. Tarabas stayed where he was, whilst in front of him, behind, and next to him on either side, the old audience went away and the new audiences came in. Five times he watched the programme from end to end. At last the morning came, and they closed the theatre.

3

IT had rained in the night. The morning was cool, the pavements were still wet. But they dried quickly in the rough, steady morning breeze. The water-wagons were already rattling through the streets, sprinkling them again.

Tarabas resolved to give himself up to the first policeman he met. As, however, for the moment, none came along, he reflected that he would do better to accost not the first but the third, on account of the figure three which had always brought him good luck. It was, indeed, more than likely that this would decide whether the café-owner was alive or dead.

The first policeman was going in the same direction as Tarabas and overtook him. This could not be called meeting him; for Tarabas "meeting" meant a face-to-face encounter. But here was one, swinging his baton, tired at the end of an all-night beat, yawning—but the first. In order to postpone the meeting with the second as long as possible, Tarabas turned into the next side street he came to—where he immediately met him, a cheerful, youthful-looking one, as though his day's duty had only just begun. Tarabas smiled at him and turned back the way he had come. It was not the law, which might be on his trail already, that he feared, but that the prophecy might be fulfilled sooner than he had thought.

"Now there's only one more left," thought Tarabas, "and then it will all be in God's hands!"

He had returned to the thoroughfare, but for a whole half-hour not another policeman appeared. Tarabas found himself actually longing for the third one to come. But at the very moment when, at the farthest end and in the middle of the broad street he emerged —the grey helmet sharp and high against the deep green of the park—at that moment the clear voice of one of New York's earliest newsboys rang out. "War between Austria and Russia!" it bugled. "War between Austria and Russia!" "War between Austria and Russia!"

One of the freshest papers—it was still damp with the dew of the morning and the printer's ink of the night—Tarabas purchased. "War between Austria and Russia!" he read.

The policeman came up and glanced at the page fresh with the morning, reading over Tarabas's shoulder.

"It's war," said Tarabas to the policeman; "I am going to fight in that war!"

"Be sure you come back alive then!" said the policeman, raising his hand to his helmet as he moved off.

Tarabas ran after him and asked the quickest way to the Russian Embassy. The information given, he set off with long strides towards the Embassy, towards the war. And Katharina, the café-owner, and his misdeed were gone from his mind and forgotten.

4

IN the presence of the mighty harbour of New York
and the great liners in their bridal white; in the unceasing monotone of dark waves beating against planks
and stone; in the tide of porters, sailors, port-officials,
onlookers, pedlars, Nicholas Tarabas completely lost all
memory of the previous day. The hearts of foolish,
easily intoxicated people are impenetrable. They are
dark wells in which thought and feeling, memory,
fear, and hope, yes, and remorse itself, can drown, and
for a while even the fear of God. Lightless and fathom-
less, a true well, was the heart of Nicholas Tarabas.
But in his large, clear eyes shone innocence.

Nevertheless—as he went on board he bought all the
newspapers within his reach at the last moment, to
find out whether any of them contained a report about
the murder by one Tarabas of the owner of a certain
café. It was as though he expected to find a notice of
an event which he alone had witnessed. More important seemed to him the ship, the cabin he would now
inhabit, the strange passengers the ship would be carrying to their destinations as it would carry him to his,
the war, and home. For he was going to the fields of

home, to the bright trilling of the larks, the whisper
of the crickets, the fragrance of potatoes roasting in the
open, the birchen fence that bound his father's house
like a plaited silver ring; to his father whom he had
thought cruel before but whom he longed now to see
again. In two great grizzled halves his father's moustache lay across his mouth, a mighty chain of harsh
hair, many times daily combed and brushed, nature's
insignia of domestic omnipotence. The mother was
gentle and blond. The father's darlings had been the
twelve-year-old Lusia, and Cousin Maria, the daughter
of the uncle who had died young and very rich. Fifteen
years of age she had been, pretty and quarrelsome,
often at odds with Nicholas Tarabas. All these things
were still far off and not yet visible, but he could feel
them plainly, beyond the crests of the ocean's dark-
green waves, and farther still, where it arched towards
the sky to become one with it.

In the newspapers there was nothing about a murdered café-owner. Tarabas threw them all together into
the sea. Probably the man had not died. It had been
nothing but a harmless brawl. In New York and in
all the world there are thousands of such every day.
Tarabas, watching the wind and water sweep the newspapers away, told himself that this was the end of
America for good and all. A little later he remembered
Katharina. He had been good to her, and she had
meant home for him—and had lied to him but once.

In that moment Tarabas was happy. (Happiness alone
could waken generosity in him.) Let her see, he said
to himself, what sort of man I am, and what she has
lost in me. She'll miss me and want me back again;
perhaps, if what she said was true, she might go home
to her sick father. But she shall grieve for me in either
case! And he went in and wrote a line to Katharina.
He expected her to stay faithful to him. He was sending money. And he did, in fact, send fifty rubles, the
half of what the Embassy had given him for his passage.

Relieved, and with a faint sense of pride, he then
applied himself to the diversions of life on board ship:
he played cards with strangers, carried on meaningless
conversations, cast frequent covetous glances towards
the pretty women, and when he found himself talking
to one of them he did not forget to mention that he
was going to the war as a lieutenant in the Russian re-
serve. Here and there he thought he caught an answering look of admiration in the women's eyes—and of
promise. But he let it rest at that. The voyage agreed
with him. His appetite was prodigious, his sleep excellent. He drank a great deal of whisky and brandy.
One could manage both a great deal better at sea than
on dry land.

Tanned, and filled with new strength, curious to see
his country once again and eager for the war, Tarabas
left the ship one morning at the port of Riga.

5

HE had to join up at Kherson where his regiment was being assembled. Two other young men left the ship together with him, soldiers, officers. He had not seen them during the voyage. Now he asked them whether they too were going to join their regiment. Yes, they said, they were on their way to the garrison in St. Petersburg; they themselves were, however, from Kiev. Once one was in the regiment, who knew whether there would be any home leave given. So they were going to see their people first, and would report for duty afterwards. They advised him to do likewise.

Tarabas saw the sense of their advice. The war had now acquired a family resemblance to death. Who could tell whether there would be any home leave, the two had said. In Tarabas's room at home, in the closet, hung the uniform he loved, loved in much the same way as father, mother, sister, and the house where he was born. Thanks to his connexions and his money, old Tarabas had succeeded in an appeal to the Tsar, and procured a lieutenancy for his son—not more than a few months after the unfortunate trial had been forgotten. Nicholas Tarabas had taken this lightly and as a matter of course. In his own opinion it was he who did the Tsar the favour of serving as lieutenant in his ninety-third infantry regiment. The Russian army would have suffered serious damage by the degradation of a Tarabas to the ranks.

So Tarabas boarded the train which carried him to his own district. He sent no word ahead. He loved to experience and to spring surprises. He would come home as a deliverer! How frightened they must be, so near the border! Victory and security would come with him!

Light of heart, Tarabas settled himself in the overcrowded train, gave the conductor an astounding tip, explained that he was a "special courier" on an important mission, fastened the latch of the compartment door, and basked in the sight of the fellow-travellers who, with a perfect right to share his compartment, were nevertheless obliged to stand in the corridor outside. Extraordinary times these; it was the people's duty to conduct themselves accordingly and to allow a courier-in-extraordinary of the Tsar the comfort indispensable to him on his important errand. From time to time Tarabas went out into the corridor. He let his eyes droop superciliously upon the poor souls he was forcing to stand, made the tired ones who had made seats out of their up-turned luggage stand up and make room for him, and was gratified to note how all of them obeyed his lightning-blue glance without a murmur, and even looked at him with a certain approbation. With unnecessary sternness he commanded the conductor, loudly so that all might hear, to make him tea and fetch this and that from the stations. Sometimes he tore open his compartment door and complained that the passengers in the corridor were making too much noise with their talk. And indeed the moment they caught sight of him they broke off and were quiet.

Delighted and amused at his own cleverness and at the others' stupidity, Nicholas Tarabas left the train the following morning after a sound and undisturbed night's sleep. Hardly two versts separated him now from his father's house. At any rate the station-master, the ticket-collector, and the porters recognized and greeted him. He answered their numerous and friendly questions with official portentousness to the effect that he had been recalled from America by orders from the highest places and for an errand of the most vital urgency. This sentence he kept repeating again and again with the same warm smile and the same bright candour in his child-like blue eyes. When this and that one asked him if he had announced his coming at home, Tarabas put his finger to his lips. The gesture exhorted silence and awoke respect. And as, without luggage, exactly as he was when he left New York, he left the station and set off down the narrow path which

led to the Tarabas demesne, the station employees, one
after the other, laid their fingers on their lips exactly
as he had done and all of them were firmly convinced
that Nicholas Tarabas, known to them since his baby-
hood, was now the bearer of a momentous state secret.

Nicholas arrived at the house at an hour when he
knew the family would be assembled at the midday
meal. In order to carry out his "surprise" to the full, he
did not take the wide road which led to the house,
accompanied on either side by the delicate, slim birch
trees he had missed so; he went by the narrow path
along the swamps. Isolated willows were trustworthy
fingerposts showing him the way which approached
the house in a semi-circle from the rear, and ended
underneath the window of his own room. It was a
gable room. A wild grapevine, well on in years, climbed
the wall strongly to the grey roof-slates with its firm
and supple arms interwoven with thick wire. To ignore
the stairs and mount the vine was an easy matter for
Tarabas, and no less easy would he find it to open his
window—should he find it closed—with a twist of
the hand learnt in boyhood, which loosened and then
pushed it open noiselessly. He took off his shoes and put
them in his coat pockets, as he had done since childhood. Nimble and silent he climbed up the wall to his
old room again. The window happened to be open; a
moment later he was in the room. He slipped to the
door and shot the bolt. The key was still in the closet.

One had to lean one's shoulder softly against it to prevent its creaking. Now it was open. The uniform hung neatly upon hangers. Tarabas took off his civilian clothes. He put on the uniform. With swift fingers he released the sword from its paper wrapping. The belt buckle snapped to—Tarabas was accoutred. He went on tip-toe down the stairs, knocked at the dining-room door, and went in.

They were in their accustomed places, father and mother, his sister and his cousin Maria. They were eating kasha.

His first greeting was for the long-missed, steaming scent of this dish, the scent of fried onions but also of blissful memories of field and grain gathered to an aromatic cloud. For the first time since he had left the ship he was conscious of hunger. Behind the faint vapour that rose from the well-filled bowl in the centre of the table the faces of his family showed dimly. It was seconds later that Tarabas noticed their astonishment, and heard the clatter of spoons put down, and the noise of chairs pushed back. Old Tarabas was the first to rise. He opened his arms. Nicholas hastened towards him, and could not help remarking two or three grains of kasha upon his father's moustache. The sight of them considerably lessened the son's tenderness. After loud kisses had been exchanged between them, Nicholas turned to greet his mother, who had just risen with a sob; then his sister who had left her

place and come round the table to reach him, and
lastly his cousin Maria, coming towards him more
slowly in her turn. Nicholas embraced her.

"I'd never have known you again," he said to Maria.

Through the strong stuff of his uniform he felt her
warm breast. In that moment his desire for his cousin
Maria was so violent and impatient that he forgot his
hunger. Her cool pursed lips no more than brushed his
cheek. Old Tarabas drew up a chair and bade his son
sit at his right hand. Nicholas sat down. He was once
more hungry for kasha, but looking at his cousin again
he felt ashamed of this.

"Have you eaten anything?" asked his mother.

"No!" said Nicholas—he almost shouted it.

They pushed plate and spoon towards him. Whilst
he ate, and told them how he had arrived and climbed
unseen up to his room, and how he had changed his
clothes there, he watched his cousin. She was strongly
built, thick-set almost, for a girl. At once tamed and
untame, her two brown plaits hung over her shoulders
and met beneath the table-cloth, probably in her lap.
Sometimes she took her hands off the table and played
with the ends of her plaits. Striking in her young and
indifferent, expressionless peasant face were only the
eyelashes. They were soft, silky, and black, very long
and curving, frail curtains over the grey half-shut eyes.
A sturdy silver crucifix lay on her breast. "Sin," thought

Tarabas; the cross excited him. It was a holy sentinel
before Maria's alluring bosom.

Tarabas in his uniform looked handsome; broad-
shouldered, narrow-hipped. They asked him to tell
them about America. They waited; he was silent. They
began to talk about the war. Old Tarabas said that it
would last three weeks. Not every soldier fell, and, as
for officers, certainly not many of them would die.
Now his mother began to weep again, but to this old
Tarabas paid not the least attention. As though it belonged to the attributes of a mother to shed tears while
others ate and talked, he held forth discursively upon
the weakness of the enemy and the strength of the
Russians, and not for one moment did he guess that
the haggard hands of death were folded already over
the whole land and over Nicholas too, his son. Dense
and deaf was old Tarabas. The mother wept.

The fence of birch rods stood round the yard and
orchard as of old. It was the season of the apple har-
vest, with the lads shaking the trees into which the
maids had clambered high among the branches to
pluck the fruit and to be seen the better by those below.
They lifted their glowing red skirts and showed their
strong white calves and thighs. Late swallows flew in
big triangular flocks towards the south. The larks
were trilling still, invisible in the sky. The windows
were open. And one heard the lancinating song of the

scythes—the last blades were being cut in all the fields, and in haste, his father told him. For the peasants were being called up, tomorrow, the day after, or in another week's time.

To the homecomer it seemed that it all came to him from infinitely far away. He could not understand why home and countryside, father and mother, had been so much nearer to him in the remoteness of that New York of stone than here. He had come back to embrace them and feel them close to his heart again. Tarabas was disappointed. They would greet him as the prodigal returned, as their deliverer, the hero—that was how his imagination had painted the scene. Their welcome was too casual. His mother had wept, but that was her nature, Tarabas said to himself. The mother he used to see in New York was different, desperate and more tender, the kind of mother his vain child's heart had need of. Could it be that during his long absence the household of Tarabas had grown used to being without its only son? He had wanted to surprise them; he had got in through the window, still in a boy's harmless fun he had put on his uniform and gone into the dining-room as though America had never been. But to them it had seemed the most ordinary thing in the world that he should suddenly be there again.

He ate on, his feelings hurt, silently and with undisturbed appetite. Without a word he carried spoonful after spoonful to his mouth, and felt that it was not he himself eating but someone else feeding him. At last he was satisfied. With a look towards Maria he said:

"Well, I'll be off again tomorrow morning. I must report the day after tomorrow at the latest."

Were they asking him to stay a while longer? Nothing of the sort!

"Very well, very well!" said his father.

His mother sobbed a little harder. His sister was unmoved. Maria cast down her eyes. The big crucifix shone upon her breast. At last they left the table.

In the afternoon Tarabas paid a few visits, to the priest, to neighbours. He had the carriage brought round. In the full glory of his uniform, splendid in blue and silver, he drove through the green and yellow of the autumn, not yet entirely at home in it all. He clicked his tongue to animate the horses, and everywhere he stopped he brought them round in an elegant and dashing sweep, tightening the reins, and they halted short and stood like bronze horses on a monument. That had always been Tarabas's way. All the small farmers greeted him. Windows opened for him as he passed, leaving a great cloud of sunlit dust behind. He enjoyed the drive and the respect that everyone was showing him. But none the less he thought he saw a great and unfamiliar fear in all their faces. The war had not yet begun, but already the terror of it had taken up its dwelling in the people's hearts. They tried

to say agreeable things to Tarabas, but it was a painful
effort, and they kept much back that they were feeling.
Tarabas was a stranger in his country—it had become
the home of war.

Evening fell. Tarabas was reluctant to go home. He
drove with slackened reins, letting the horses take
their dreamy pace. When he came to the avenue of
birches which led up to the house, he descended. The
horses knew their way. They would go straight to the
big stables to the left of the house and stop there; saga-
ciously they would announce themselves by whinnying, and the watch-dog would start barking if the
groom did not come at once. Only the horses had really
welcomed Tarabas. He felt how much he loved them.
He stroked the shining chestnut bodies, hot after the
drive, laid his forehead against each one's forehead, in-
haled the vapour from their nostrils'and felt the good
coolness of their leathern skin. All the love in the world
seemed to him to shine out of their large eyes.

For the second time that day he took the by-path
where the willows grew. The frogs sent forth their
din on either side; it smelt like rain, although the sky
was clear of clouds and the autumn sun was going
down in brightness to a clear horizon. It dazzled him.
He had to keep his eyes upon the path before him so as
not to take a false step. Thus he did not see that somebody was coming towards him. A shadow close before
his feet surprised him; he guessed instantly to whom it

belonged, and stopped. Maria was coming down the
path. She had missed him, then. She set her high-laced
boots daintily and carefully one before the other along
the narrow path. Suddenly Tarabas was seized with a
desire to slit the intricate lacings open. A rage of passion filled him. There was no help for it now. He let
Maria come. He put one arm round her. They walked,
pressed hard against each other, and carefully, for fear
of the swamp on either side, and out of the homesickness that was in them; their feet touched sometimes on
the narrow path. They turned back, into the wood.
Late birds were calling. They spoke no word. Suddenly
they embraced. They turned, both at the same moment,
towards each other, were locked in each other's arms,
staggered, and sank down upon the ground.

When they stood up again, the stars were gleaming
through the tree-tops. It was chilly. Clinging together,
they returned to the house along the avenue. At the
door they stopped and exchanged long kisses, as though
their parting was for ever.

"You go in first," said Tarabas. These were the only
words that either had said in all the time.

Tarabas followed slowly.

The family assembled for supper. The elder Tarabas
asked his son when he would have to leave. At four
o'clock in the morning, said Nicholas, so as to be quite
certain not to miss the train. Just as he had reckoned it
out himself, said the old man.

The special meal which the father had ordered in the afternoon was now brought in—a steaming milk-porridge, boiled pork and potatoes, vodka and a light Burgundy in between, white sheep's cheese at the end. The talk grew loud. The old man asked many questions. Nicholas told about America. On the spur of the moment he invented a factory in which he had just begun to work. A film factory; typically American. At five o'clock one morning, the hour at which he had been going to his work for weeks, he heard the newsboys shouting the news about the war. And so he had gone straight to the Russian Embassy. One evening before that there had been a fight between himself, Tarabas, and the owner of a café, a vile fellow. He had insulted and even maltreated an innocent girl, probably a waitress in the café. You came across such people in New York.

Even the nonchalant sister's attention was won by this story, and his mother kept repeating: "God bless you, my boy!" Nicholas himself was convinced that he had been telling the perfect truth.

And then they all got up. The farewell was celebrated standing. And old Tarabas said that they would see their son again in four weeks' time. And they all kissed him. Tomorrow morning he would rather not see anyone. Maria's kiss was light. His mother held him a while in her arms, swaying backwards and forwards with him as they stood. Perhaps she was remembering the time when she had rocked him in her lap. The servants came. With each one, men and maids, Nicholas exchanged the kiss of parting.

He went up to his room. He lay down as he was, with the wet mud still on his boots, upon the bed. He must have been asleep an hour when an unfamiliar sound woke him; he saw that his door was open and went to close it. The window opposite was open too.

He could not get to sleep again. It occurred to him that it could not have been merely the wind. Had Maria wanted to meet him again? He knew her room. She lay there in her nightdress now, and the crucifix hung above her bed. It frightened him a little.

He opened the door. He slid down the banisters with both hands so as not to tread upon the stairs with his heavy boots. Now he was opening Maria's door. He bolted it behind him. He stood there for a moment without sound or movement. There was the bed; he knew it well. As a boy he and Maria and his sister had often pulled the sheets off it to play funeral processions. Each had been the corpse in turn. Through the wide square of the window shone the clear blue night. Tarabas approached the bed. The floor creaked, and Maria started up. Still half asleep and wholly terrified, she opened her arms. She received Tarabas as he was, booted and clad, felt with rapture the roughness of his unshaven face against her own, and groped for his neck with awkward hands.

Appeased, domineering and noisy, he got up. Maria's hands, which she stretched out towards him still, he laid back on the coverlet, gently but with a faint touch of impatience.

"You're mine!" said Tarabas. "When I come back we'll get married. And you'll be faithful to me; don't you look at another man while I'm away. Good-bye!" —And he left the room. Careless of the noise he made, he went upstairs to fetch his things.

He found his father in his room. "Spying on me," the thought flashed into Nicholas's mind. "I'm being spied on." The old fierce resentment against his father woke again, the resentment against the old man who had cruelly driven him from home out into the cruelty of New York. Old Tarabas rose; his dressing-gown gaped open, showing the peasant shirt and the long tubes of the underpants tied at the massive ankles. With both hands the father seized Nicholas by the epaulettes.

"I degrade you!" he said. Oh, that was a voice one knew of old, it was no louder than usual. Only the Adam's apple rose and fell more violently than otherwise—and cold fury stood in the eyes, clear, icy fury.

"Something's going to happen now," Nicholas said to himself, and fear for his epaulettes bewildered him.

"Let go!" he shouted. The next moment the paternal hand had struck him savagely across the cheek.

Nicholas fell back; the old man put his dressing-gown to rights.

"If nothing happens to you in the war, you marry!" said old Tarabas. "Now go! At once! Get out!"

Nicholas Tarabas seized his sword and coat and turned to go. He opened the door, paused a moment, turned back again and spat. Then he slammed the door behind him and hastened out of the house. Horses, coachman, and carriage were already waiting to take him to the station.

6

THE war became his home. The war became his wide and bloody home. He moved from one sector to another. He came to peaceful territory, set villages on fire, left the debris of smaller and larger towns behind him, and mourning women, orphaned children, beaten, hanged, and murdered men. He turned about, learnt the suspense of flight before the enemy, took last-minute revenge on supposed traitors, destroyed bridges, roads, railways, obeyed and commanded, and all with equal relish. He was the bravest officer in his regiment. He led patrols with the caution and cunning of a beast of prey out for booty, and with the confident daring of a foolish man to whom his life means nothing. He drove his timorous peasants to the attack with pistol and whip, but fired the brave ones with his own example.—He was first into everything. In the art of invisible motion, when, masked by trees, shrubs, or undergrowth, covered by darkness or wrapped in the mists of dawn, he would steal upon barbed-wire barricades to the undoing of the enemy, he was unequalled. He never needed to look at any map; his whetted senses divined the secrets of every territory. Muffled and distant sounds came clearly to his ears. His watchful eye caught every suspicious movement. His certain hand went out, shot, and never missed its mark, held what it grasped, came down without mercy upon backs and faces, shut to a fist with cruel knuckles, but opened readily to the pressure of comradeship, answering it with warmth and steel. Tarabas liked none but his own kind. He was mentioned in dispatches and promoted to captain. Whoever in his company showed a tendency to hesitate, let alone a hint of cowardice, he was Tarabas's enemy, no different from the enemy against whom the whole army was at war. But whoever, like Tarabas, held his life cheap and had no fear of death, he was the friend of his bosom. Hunger and thirst, pain and fatigue, days and nights sleepless on the march, strengthened his heart, rejoiced it even. Failing utterly to give proof of strategic talent, and incapable of comprehending what in military idiom is called "larger actions," he was an extraordinary front officer, an admirable hunter on a small ground. Yes, he was a hunter, a wild hunter was Nicholas Tarabas.

He became acquainted with heavy drinking and light loving. Forgotten were house and home, father and mother and Cousin Maria. When one day he remembered them again, it was too late to send them any news, for by that time Tarabas's home was in possession of the enemy. Little he cared; the war had become his vast and bloody home. Forgotten were New York and Katharina. And yet in many a pause between danger and fighting, drunkenness and sobriety, passing intoxication and passing murder, for seconds together —though for seconds only—it became clear to him that ever since the hour in which the gipsy had told his fortune at that Coney Island booth he had lived like one transformed, transformed and bewitched, like one caught in the toils of a dream. Ah, this was not his own life any more!—At times it seemed to him that he had died, and that the life he led was taking place in the beyond. But these seconds of reflection were no sooner come than gone again, and Tarabas went down once more into the narcosis of blood that flowed all round him and that he caused to flow, the odour of dead bodies, the incendiary smoke-clouds, and his love of ruin and destruction.

And so he went, so let himself be ordered, from fire to fire, from murder to murder, and neither hurt nor harm befell him. A higher power kept watch over him and preserved him to live his strange life out. His men loved him and feared him, too. His glance was a command, and the least gesture of his hand. And when it happened that one among them revolted at some act of Tarabas's cruelty, scarcely a single comrade stood by the malcontent. They all loved Tarabas; and none but was afraid of him.

And Tarabas loved his men, he loved his men in his own fashion, because he was their lord and master. He saw many of them die. He liked it. He liked to have men die all round him, and when, in the intervals between the onslaughts, he went—the only one in all the regiment to do so—through the trenches calling the roll of his men, and the answer "Fallen" came, he marked it with a cross in his note-book. At such moments he enjoyed the fancy that he himself was dead, that all the happenings amongst which he moved were taking place in the beyond, and that the others, the fallen, had passed as certainly into a third life as he into this second.

He was not once wounded or once sick; he never asked for leave. He was the only one in the regiment who neither received mail nor expected any. His home he never mentioned. And this confirmed the general opinion that there was something very strange about him.

Thus he spent the war.

When the revolution broke out, he kept his company savagely in hand, by looks and gestures, fists, pistol, and stick. It was not for him to understand what politics had brought to pass. It did not disturb him that the Tsar had been deposed. In his troop he was the Tsar. It could only please him when his superior officers, the staff and general headquarters, began to send out confused and contradictory orders. He need pay the less attention to them. Soon, because he was the only one in all the regiment whom the revolution had not bewildered or transformed, he acquired more power than the colonel himself. He became the virtual commander of the regiment. And he transferred it hither and thither as he thought fit, went into independent scrimmages, broke into unoffending villages and townlets, cheerful and fresh as in the first weeks of the war.

One day—it was a Sunday—there appeared in his regiment a soldier he had never seen before. For the first time since he had seen service he felt a shock, and the cause of it was a simple, ordinary private. They were encamped in a tiny Galician village, half shot to pieces but with a few cottages still fairly intact. In one of these Captain Tarabas had spent the night with the peasant woman's fourteen-year-old daughter, and in the morning had ordered his servant to bring him coffee and brandy. It was a sunny day, about nine o'clock in the morning. In freshly polished boots and wide riding-breeches, brushed and cleaned, riding-crop in hand, shaved and equipped with all the sense of well-being that could fill a man like Tarabas on a brilliant autumn morning after a thoroughly agreeable night, the captain left the hut and the girl, who was crouching at the door in her chemise. Tarabas tapped her on the shoulder gently with his riding-switch. The girl rose. He asked her what her name was.

"You asked me last night what my name was, Master," she said, "when I came into bed."

She had tiny green eyes deeply imbedded in the cheeks; a mischievous and wicked spark burnt in them. Tarabas saw her young bosom underneath her shift, and a thin chain round her neck. He thought of the crucifix Maria had worn and said, touching her head with his whip: "Your name's Maria from now on, as long as I stay here!"

"Yes, Master!" said the girl.

And Tarabas went away whistling.

He was in excellent spirits. He tried to disperse the glistening strands of the gossamers with the handle of his crop. He did not succeed; the mysterious creatures made of nothing wound themselves, on the contrary, round the handle, positively caressing it. That too pleased Tarabas. Thereupon he made himself a cigarette, taking the tobacco loose out of his pocket, and slackened his pace. He was nearing his men's encampment. The sergeant was already coming towards him to report. It was Sunday. The soldiers lay about on the sloping meadows and in the mown fields, lazy and inert.

"Stay where you are!" called Tarabas as he neared them. One, however, rose from his place at the edge of the road, one nearest Tarabas. And although this soldier saluted as prescribed, stiff and immovable as a post and with extreme deference even, the captain found something insubordinate and insolent, some-

thing incomprehensibly superior in the whole figure of
the man. No, he had not been trained in Tarabas's
school! This was a stranger in the company!

Tarabas came on—and instantly stepped back. At
that moment the bell of the little Greek church began
to ring. The first peasant women appeared upon the
road that led to the church. Today was Sunday. Tarabas crossed himself, still with his eyes fixed upon the
strange soldier. And it was as though he had crossed
himself in fear of him. For in that instant he had seen
distinctly that the strange soldier was a red-haired
Jew. A red-haired Jew. Red-haired, Jew—and it was
Sunday!

For the first time since he was in the army his old
superstitiousness awoke in Tarabas. He knew at once
that from that moment on his life would undergo a
change.

"How did you come here?" asked Tarabas. The soldier pulled a paper out of his pocket, by which one saw
that he had come from the fifty-second infantry regiment, which had been wiped out, partly through desertions and partly by going over to the Bolsheviki.

"All right!" said Captain Tarabas. "Are you a Jew?"

"Yes," said the soldier. "My parents were Jews. But
I don't believe in God!"

Nicholas Tarabas fell back another step. He beat
against his high boot with his riding-whip. The red-

headed man had grey-green eyes and short flaming
bushes over them instead of eyebrows.

"So that's what you are!" said the captain. "An atheist! Hm! Hm!"

He went on. The soldier lay down again on the edge
of the road. Tarabas turned round once only. He saw
the stranger's red hair; it shone out amidst the meagre
grass of the slope, a little fire on the grey and dusty
highway.

7

FROM that very day the world of Captain Tarabas began to undergo a change. His men no longer obeyed him as before; they seemed to like him less and fear him less. And when he chastised any one of them, he felt an indefinable, invisible, inaudible resentment go through the ranks. The men no longer looked him straight in the face. One day two of his non-commissioned officers vanished, the best men in the regiment, at whose side he had fought since his first day in the field. A private or two followed them a week later. But the red-haired atheist did not leave, the only one whose desertion the captain ardently desired. He was certainly a faultless soldier. He was punctual and obedient. But Captain Tarabas seldom gave him any order. The others felt it. Yes, they knew. Sometimes Tarabas watched the red-haired one talking to the soldiers. They listened to him, surrounded him, hung on his words. Tarabas would then call one of them at random to him.

"What is he telling you, that red-headed one?"

"Stories, sir!" the soldier would answer.

"What sort of stories?"

"Oh, funny ones, sir—about women!"

And Tarabas knew the man was lying. But he was ashamed that he had been lied to, and asked no further questions.

One morning the captain found among his orderly's things something he had never set eyes on until then, a Bolshevist pamphlet. He put a match to it; the pages burnt only half-way and then the flame went out. Tarabas threw it down. Thereafter he kept a more watchful eye upon his servant.

"Stepan," he would say, "have you nothing to tell me?—Where is your mouth-organ, Stepan, wouldn't you like to give me a tune?"

"Lost it, sir!" Stepan would answer, humble and sad.

And one evening Stepan, too, disappeared without warning. No one knew anything about it.

Captain Tarabas had the whole lot line up and called the roll. More than half were gone. He put the remnant through an hour's drill. The red-haired private drilled sturdily, unshirkingly, immaculately, a faultless soldier.

A day or so later, at the hour when Tarabas, the colonel, and the other officers sat in council discussing how to cope with the desertions, the red-haired one appeared, two hand-grenades in his belt and a pistol in his hand, accompanied by two non-commissioned officers.

"Citizens," said the red-haired atheist, "the revolution has triumphed. Give up your arms, you will be given safe conduct. You, Citizen Tarabas, and whatever other countrymen of yours are here, can go back home. Your people there have got their own government; it's an independent country now."

It was very quiet. The only sound was the ticking of the colonel's big watch which lay open on the table; stitching time like a sewing-machine.

8

WHEN the red-haired soldier had left the room with his men, the colonel got up and stood a while as though meditating some plan, as though, in the hour which had sealed the army's, the regiment's, and his own doom, a saving revelation had been vouchsafed him. Tarabas looked up from his chair with a questioning glance. The colonel turned away. He pushed his arm-chair back. The solid, leather-upholstered back met the plank floor with a thud. The colonel went over to the window. His broad back almost filled the wide frame. Tarabas did not move. Suddenly a sob broke from the colonel's throat. It sounded like a short, abrupt, and quickly stifled cry, strange, as though it came not from the colonel's throat but directly out of his heart; yes, as though the heart possessed its own quite special throat through which it cried its special pain into the world. The massive shoulders rose and fell for the space of a second. Then the old man turned round again and went back to the table. He stood a while looking at the big open watch ticking away with pitiless regularity; he gazed intently at it as though he had never before seen the swift circuit of the fine hand that marked the seconds. Tarabas too looked at the watch. Nothing stirred in him; his head was empty, his heart had gone cold. He thought he heard it beating, ticking in time with the watch upon the table. There was no other sound in the room. It seemed to Tarabas that a very long time had passed since the red-haired one had left them there. At last the colonel spoke.

"Tarabas," he said, "I'd like to give you this watch as a memento."

The colonel took out his pen-knife and opened the back. He read the inscription engraved in Russian characters: "To my son, Ossip Ivanovich Kudra," and showed it to Tarabas.

"I got this watch on leaving the cadets' school. My father was very proud of me. I was proud myself. I come of very humble people. My father's father was still a serf on the Tsaritsyns' estate. I've never been much of a soldier, Captain Tarabas. I've been lazy and negligent, I think. We've always had a lot of officers like that. Will you do me the honour of accepting the watch, Brother Tarabas?"

"I'll take it," said Tarabas, rising.

The colonel shut both covers of the watch and handed it across the table to Tarabas. He still stood there for a while, his grey head bowed down. Then he said: "Excuse me, I'll just go and get my things!" went

slowly round the table, past Tarabas, to the door, and
went out. The next moment there was a shot. At once
Tarabas said to himself: "That's he!" He opened the
door. The colonel lay at full length just outside. He
must have laid himself down deliberately and then
shot. His coat was open. The blood was soaking
through the shirt. The dead man's hands were still
warm. The index finger still held the trigger. Tarabas
took the weapon away. Then he folded the colonel's
hands across his breast.

A few soldiers came up and stood round the corpse
and the kneeling Tarabas. They took off their caps;
it was not clear to them what they were doing there,
but they remained.

Tarabas stood up.

"We'll bury him at once, here, in front of the house,"
he ordered. "Dig a grave! Then line up. With rifles!
Call Kontsev!"

Sergeant-Major Kontsev came. "I've only twenty-six
men left, sir," he said.

"Line them up!" commanded Tarabas.

They buried the colonel two hours later, ten paces
from the door of the house. Twenty-six men, the faithful remnant of the regiment, fired three times into the
air at Tarabas's command.

Six pitiable ranks formed fours and faced about.

But Tarabas at their head marched as though he led

an unscathed, intact regiment; he had by no means
decided to admit that his world was destroyed or the
war ended.

   With his twenty-six men, some of whom were from
the same part of the country as he, Tarabas started out
for home, for the new chief city of the new state.
Brand-new ministers, governors, and generals had been
appointed there, and in all haste a small provisional
army was being formed. Everywhere was turmoil—
between the inhabitants and those in power, and among
the latter themselves, there was nothing but confusion. Tarabas, however, filled with insatiable lust for
adventure and with an honest, ardent hatred for the
many offices and officials, bureaux and documents, was
determined that his career had not yet reached its end.
He was a soldier, nothing else. He had his trusty
twenty-six, for whom, as for himself, the war had been
the only home they knew, and to whom, as to himself,
he owed a new home now. To make these twenty-six
the nucleus of a whole new regiment—what a mission
for a Tarabas! He was not the man to take his own
life like the good old colonel. History, chipping small
new countries that men should live and die for off the
big old ones which they had lived and died for until
then—history was no concern of Tarabas. As long as
he lived he would refuse to recognize the so-called
inevitable course of events. He was responsible to his

twenty-six. What was the new War Minister of a new country to him? Less than any private in his company! He betook himself to the War Minister, splendidly equipped, heavily armed, followed by his twenty-six; ushers, clerks, and secretaries who asked him his errand he browbeat with his thundered orders, mightier in the ante-room than the minister himself. In this personage, however, the first few words sufficed to reveal to him a kinsman of his mother's family.

As the obvious and no more than adequate reward for his military services Tarabas asked for the command of one of the new home regiments about to be formed. This desire of the captain's, emphatically supported by his violent and domineering manner, by the pistol and the riding-crop, to say nothing of the impression which his retinue made upon the minister, took barely two hours to fulfil. Thus out of the ruins of the old army Captain Tarabas emerged a colonel. He was charged with the formation of a new regiment in the garrison of Koropta.

9

THE little town of Koropta was in the throes of utmost bewilderment when Tarabas and his henchmen arrived. It was filled with men in the most various uniforms, swarmed hither and cast up from every section of the front and from the interior of the land; prisoners from the suddenly abandoned camps, vagrants and drunkards, many lured by the chance of exploiting the general chaos to some adventurous profit of their own, there to tempt fortune while they might, and Providence as well. They roamed about in the narrow streets, camped in the broad desolate square of the market-place, perched upon farm-wagons and army automobiles as they rolled aimlessly about, squatted on the sunlit steps of the big court-house or on the old gravestones in the cemetery on the hill. At the summit of this hill arose the small bright yellow church of the town.

It was a clear and perfect autumn day. In its matchless azure brilliance the dilapidated little houses with their crooked shingled roofs, the wooden sidewalks, the dried-out, silver-gleaming mud between, the ragged uniforms—all looked like a splendid painting in con-

tinuous movement; the figures and all its separate parts
seemed to be still in search of their final place in it.
In amongst the coloured uniforms flitted the quick,
fearsome shadows of Jews in long caftans, and the
light-yellow sheepskins of the peasant men and women.
Women with variegated flowered kerchiefs on their
heads sat on the low thresholds in the open doorways
of the little houses, engaged in purposeless, agitated
chatter. The children played in the middle of the street.
And through the silvery slush ducks and geese waded
towards such black puddles as had happily not yet
been dried up by the sun.

Amidst this scene of peace the poor inhabitants of
Koropta were at their wits' end and terribly excited.
They lived in expectation of something dreadful, worse
perhaps than anything the war had brought them yet.
Its immense, burning boots had trodden into the poor
rows of Koropta's houses and left their blackened,
wasted track behind. The old low wall round the grave-
yard on the hill had many holes to show where senseless shots had missed their aim; there the war had
buried its murderous fingers in the stone. With those
same fingers it had lately strangled many a son of the
little town. Peaceful in their lives the people of Koropta
had always been, without a thought beyond their
meagre days and quiet nights, intent upon the simple
course of their simple destinies. Suddenly overtaken
by the war, they first stood petrified before its dreadful

face, then turned and fled before it, but turned back
again, made up their minds to stay, spellbound in its
fiery breath. They all were innocent, they knew nothing of history's murderous laws, stolid and uncom-
plaining they bore the blows God dealt them as they
had borne the Tsar's blows years without end before.
They hardly could believe the tidings that the Tsar no
longer sat upon his golden throne in St. Petersburg,
still less the second and more awful news that he had
been shot like a dog too old to be of any more use. And
now they were being told that they themselves were
no longer part of Russia, but an independent country.
Now, said the teachers, the lawyers, the educated folk,
they were a free, delivered nation. What was the meaning of such talk as this? And of what dire peril was
this tumult in their town the promise?

Captain Tarabas troubled his head as little about
the laws of history as did the inhabitants of Koropta.
The deliverance of the nation enabled him to continue
his life as a soldier. What had he to do with politics?
That was for the teachers, the lawyers, the educated
folk! Captain Tarabas was a colonel now. It was his
task to get together a first-rate regiment and to command it. No other man than Nicholas Tarabas would
have been capable of gathering a whole regiment together with a handful of men. He had a definite plan.
In the diminutive railway-station of Koropta, immediately in front of the wooden barracks, where an old

Russian major still gave orders to one non-commissioned officer and the station sentry, Tarabas drew his men up in a double row and put them through a little drill. He had them kneel down and shoulder arms, and fire a volley or two into the air, all in the presence of a few astonished spectators, some in civilian clothes and some in uniform; the station sentry and the old major were also in the audience. Tarabas, visibly gratified at the number of spectators whom the meaningless shooting had lured to watch the remarkable proceedings, thereupon addressed his company.

"You men," spoke Tarabas, "who have followed me into many battles and the rests between them, into the war against the enemy and against the revolution, you have no wish to lay down your arms now and go back peacefully to your homes. You, and I, too, we want to die as soldiers, and as soldiers only! With your help I am going to form a new regiment in this place, to serve the new country fate has given us. Fall out!"

The little troop shouldered arms. All of them were terrible to see, more terrible by far than the menacing and ragged figures on the station and about the town. For they possessed all the accoutred, rattling, clinking, spurred, and well-groomed frightfulness of their leader and master. Bright gleamed the diligently oiled rifle-barrels; the shoulder-straps were taut and strong across the broad chests and shoulders, and belted the close jackets without spot or wrinkle. Like Tarabas they all

wore martial, neatly brushed, enormous moustaches
for the adornment of their faces, sleek with good nourishment. And the eyes of all of them were cold and
hard, good, vigilant steel. Tarabas himself, although
Heaven knows his strength of purpose needed no heartening sight to feed and strengthen it still more, even
Tarabas felt his power confirmed when he looked at
those men of his. Each one of them was a faithful and
devoted image of himself. Together they were as six-
and-twenty Tarabases, six-and-twenty replicas of the
great Nicholas Tarabas, and but for him non-existent.
That is what they were, his twenty-six reflections.

He told them to wait for the time being, and strode
with clanking footsteps into the station headquarters.
He found nobody there. For the old major, likewise
his sergeant, were still outside on the platform whence
they had witnessed Tarabas's remarkable drill-parade
and the remarkable discipline of his troops. Colonel
Tarabas struck the table with his riding-crop. It was a
blow that must surely be heard all over the now silent
station. And the major appeared at once.

"I am Colonel Tarabas," said Nicholas. "I have been
charged with the formation of a regiment in this town.
I shall also be taking over the command of the town
until further orders. For the present I should be obliged
if you will inform me where I shall find billets for
myself and my twenty-six men."

The old major remained quietly beside the door

through which he had just entered. It was many a long
day since he had heard talk like this. It was the soldier's
music, familiar to him since boyhood and heard no
more since the outbreak of the revolution, a melody he
had thought never to hear again. The grey-haired major—Kisilaika was his name—felt his limbs stiffen under Tarabas's words. He felt his bones hardening, his
poor old bones; his muscles tightened and obeyed the
military language they knew.

"Very good, sir," said Major Kisilaika. "The main
barracks lie half a mile outside the town. But I'm
afraid the commissariat has run very low. I don't
know——"

"I'm not going another step," said Colonel Tarabas.
"What food there is I want brought here. Who are all
those fellows loafing about the station? Let them bring
it. I'll place a guard at each exit."

And Tarabas returned to his men.

"Nobody in this station is to leave it," cried Tarabas.

And there was general consternation. Pure curiosity
and unthinking idleness had brought them there to
gather near the strange newcomers and gaze at them.
And now they were prisoners. For a long time they
had been accustomed to bearing hunger and thirst and
privations of every kind. But freedom had been theirs.
Now at one blow even their freedom had been taken
from them. They were prisoners. They no longer even
dared to look about them. Of Tarabas's former audi-

ence one only, a little skinny civilian Jew, inspired by
timorous recklessness or the hope of God knows what
miracle, attempted to gain one of the exits. But on the
instant Tarabas shot at the fugitive—and the poor thing
fell; with a loud, unhuman bellow he fell down, hit in
the left thigh in the precise spot at which Tarabas had
aimed. The thin, bony little head with its sparse goatee
lay stretched face upwards right on the edge of a pile
of gravel which was used to show the engine-drivers
where to stop, and the wretched boots with their ripped
soles and misshapen toes pointed towards the glass
roof. Tarabas himself went over to the casualty, picked
up the feather-weight Jew, and carried him across both
arms, as he would have carried a thin little birch tree,
into the office of the station headquarters. There was
complete silence. When the report of the shot had died
away, not another sound was to be heard. It was as
though it had hit everyone there, and struck them
dumb and numb. Tarabas laid the weightless body of
his now unconscious victim on the major's paper-
strewn table, ripped up the Jew's ancient, shiny, dark-
grey trouser-leg, pulled out his own handkerchief, inspected the wound, and said to the startled major:
"Flesh-wound!" And then he called out: "Bandage!"
And one of his men who had been a hairdresser and
performed the ambulance duties to the troop came in
and began to render swift and careful first-aid to the
wounded Jew.

The paralysed spectators in the station were some forty in number. Tarabas had them lined up. He put two of his men in charge of them. They were to go and fetch food. The remainder stayed on the wide platform in the sunshine and waited. Tarabas stood at the edge of the platform and looked at the bluely gleaming, narrow, hurrying railway-tracks; meanwhile, indoors, in the major's office, the wounded Jew was coming to himself again. His thin and feeble wailing could be heard through the open door. In the blue sky sparrows twittered.

It was not long before the men came back with food. The clatter of tin vessels and the regular tramp of men's boots could be heard. They came into sight. The distribution of the meal began. The first bowlful was for Tarabas. In the midst of the opaque grey soup rose a piece of dark-brown meat like a rock out of the sea. Tarabas pulled a spoon out of his boot, and at the same moment his men followed suit. The forty prisoners who had gone with them stood by and did not move or speak. Hunger dwelt in their wide eyes. The water gathered in their mouths. The busy clatter of tin spoons against the bowls was almost more than they could bear. Some of them tried, by putting their fingers in their ears, to shut out the sound. Tarabas was the first to put down his spoon. To the prisoner standing nearest him he handed the rest of his meal, together with the spoon. And, without a word from him, all his men did likewise. Each put down his bowl with a jerk and handed it to the prisoner nearest him. The whole proceeding took place without a word. There was now no sound but the clatter of tin spoons against bowls, smacking of lips, teeth chewing, and sparrows twittering under the glass roof of the station.

When everyone had eaten, Colonel Tarabas ordered the march into the town. The men who had been thus suddenly and accidentally taken prisoners found their changed situation suddenly more tolerable. They let themselves be drawn up between Tarabas's troops. And flanked by a living wall of armed soldiery they marched, contented and indifferent, many of them joyfully, under Tarabas's command into the little town of Koropta.

They marched through the half-dried silvery mud of the roads—and the geese, the ducks, and the children scattered before them with loud and frightened cries. The little regiment spread a strange terror. The townsfolk of Koropta did not know what new kind of war could now have broken out. For the march of Colonel Tarabas upon their town seemed like a new kind of war to them. Swift and terrible rumours had flown out in advance of Tarabas. He was the new king of the new country, said some. And others declared he was the son of the Tsar himself, and had come to take revenge for his father's fate.

But as for the Jews, of whom a few hundred lived

in Koropta, they were all busily occupied, this being a Friday and the Sabbath drawing near on holy feet, in shutting up their tiny shops with all possible haste, and in the firm belief that their Sabbath could place a check upon the course of history, just as it did upon their businesses.

Tarabas, at the head of his dangerous troop, did not understand why the little shops were being shut so hurriedly, and took it as a personal affront. The gossiping women got up from their doorsteps as he approached. The iron rattle of chains and bolts and padlocks on the wooden shops were heard. Here and there the dark shadow of a Jew flitted by, coming towards Tarabas, clinging to the meagre protection the houses afforded. Before his eyes and all along his route, Tarabas saw nothing but fugitives. That anyone could be afraid of him was something he could not understand. And as he marched on, care and worry gained upon him. Yes, the townlet of Koropta had care in store for him.

He halted outside the government building, mounted the broad steps, followed by two of his armed men, and opened a folding door behind which he assumed that he would find the chief of police. And there indeed he sat, a pitiful, aged man, haggard and diminutive and lost in the mighty chair of office, a figure belonging to a bygone age.

"I have taken over the command of this town," said

Tarabas. "I am to form a new regiment here. Let me
have a list of the principal buildings. Where are the
barracks? Then you had best go home."

"With pleasure," said the little old creature. And began, in a cobwebby, extraordinarily thin voice, which
seemed to come out of an antique cupboard, to recite
what had been asked of him. Then he rose. His bald,
yellowish, spotted skull hardly came up to the top of
the chair-back. He took his hat and stick from the rack,
bowed and smiled, and was gone.

"Sit down there!" said Tarabas to one of his escort.
"Until I come back, you are the chief of police!" And
Tarabas went from one of the few public departments
in Koropta to the other, making a clean sweep everywhere. Then he took possession of the empty barracks,
and talked to the assembled prisoners in the yard.

"Which of you have been soldiers?" he asked.
"Which of you want to go on being soldiers under
me?"

They all came forward. They all wanted to be soldiers under Tarabas.

10

WHEN word of the terrible Tarabas and his terrible companions reached the inn of "The White Eagle," the inn-keeper, the Jew, Nathan Kristianpoller, decided to close up his home without delay and send his wife and seven children to her parents in Kyrbitki. It was not the first time the Kristianpoller family had made that journey. It had begun with the outbreak of the war, and was repeated when a strange regiment of Cossacks had come into the town, and again when the Germans had marched in and occupied parts of western Russia. On the first journey there were five children, then six, and finally no less than seven girls and boys. For, independent of the ever-changing terrors of the war, nature continued to bestow upon the Kristianpollers her blessings, kindly but no less implacable.

The inn of "The White Eagle"—it was the only one in Koropta—had come down to the Jew, Kristianpoller, from his forefathers. For more than a hundred and fifty years Kristianpollers had owned and managed it. Nathan Kristianpoller, their heir, knew nothing of his ancestors but this. He had grown up within its thick and crumbling walls, overgrown with wild grapevines

and cracked in many places. A wide double-door
painted reddish brown at once interrupted and com-
pleted the walls' continuity, as a stone breaks and com-
pletes the circle of a ring. In that doorway the father
and grandfather of Nathan Kristianpoller had waited
and welcomed the peasants who came to the Koropta
market on Thursdays and Fridays to sell their pigs and
buy scythes and sickles, and horse-shoes, and bright
kerchiefs, of the tradesmen in the little shops. Until the
day when war broke out, the inn-keeper Kristianpoller
had had no cause to think of change. But as time went
on he very soon grew accustomed to the altered aspect
of the world, and, like many of his brethren, he contrived to avert all danger from himself and his. With
cunning and the help of God he was able to hold his
inborn and acquired wits like a shield against the soldiers of his own and other lands, and keep a whole
skin for himself and his family.

Now, however, with the arrival of the terrible Tarabas, the inn-keeper Kristianpoller became possessed
with a terror entirely foreign to his nature and unlike
any he had ever felt before. An unknown apprehension
filled his heart which had grown used to all the usual,
established fears. "Who is this Tarabas?" asked Kristianpoller's heart. Like a glittering king of steel he
comes to Koropta. New and iron troubles, full of danger, he has brought with him to Koropta. Other times
will come, and God knows what new laws! Have

mercy, Lord, upon us all, and upon Nathan Kristian-poller in particular!

For a fortnight now the officers of the new army of the new-born country had been living at the White Eagle with their servants. It is true that they caroused each night in the spacious parlour, shaking the brown rafters on the low plank ceiling with their noise which they continued in their own rooms afterwards. But Kristianpoller soon realized that their wildness and drinking had nothing worse behind it than harmless exuberance, and that they were only waiting for the call of a lord and master who would lead them to objectives still unknown but certainly full of peril. And certainly Tarabas was that lord and master. Accordingly Kristianpoller loaded his whole family, as was his wont now, into the big landau which stood in readiness in the hotel stable, and dispatched all his dear ones to Kyrbitki. He stayed behind. He forsook the two large rooms to which an almost invisible door in the tap-room gave access, and in which he and the family had lived, and made himself a shake-down of straw on the kitchen floor. Beside the shed in the yard there was a small building of yellow brick, half fallen down and, built for no apparent purpose, put only to temporary and occasional uses. It was a lumber-room for all kinds of household implements, empty barrels, tubs, and baskets, logs for the winter and bundles of kindling, old samovars no longer fit for service and all manner of

other useful and useless litter such as collects in the
course of years.

In his early youth Kristianpoller had never been able
to enter this building without a touch of fear. For there
was a tale about it to the effect that long, long ago,
when the first Christian missionaries had come to this
stubborn heathen land, in that very yard and on that
very spot they had erected a chapel. The Jew Kristianpoller kept these stories locked up in his own breast;
he did not divulge them, for something told him that
they were true. Had he been convinced that they were
merely legends he would not have been so careful never
to mention them, not even when he might well have
done so, instead of enjoining silence upon his wife and
the children whenever one of them referred to the
strange origins of their lumber-house. Such foolish tales
should not be repeated, Kristianpoller used to say.

He now gave Fedya, the stable-boy, orders to clean
out the "out-house" and put it in order. He himself
descended to the cellar, where the portly little brandy
kegs were stored, and the bigger wine barrels, which
were very old and had fortunately survived even the
war and all the subsequent invasions. The cellar was a
spacious vaulted one in two stories; it had stone walls, a
stone floor, and a steep winding staircase. Arrived upon
the last step, the foot met a large flagstone which, with
the aid of a stout iron ring, one could raise slightly and
prop open with a heavy iron bar. Kristianpoller had

taken this ring out of its hook and hidden it, in order
that no one whose business it was not should be inspired with the idea that the cellar had another story
underneath. But in that deeper level the old and costly
wines were kept. Beer and brandy were in the open
cellar, accessible to all.

The iron bar and the ring were now brought from
their hiding-place and dragged into the bar. Kristianpoller was a man of fair strength; his face and neck
were ruddy with the breath of the alcohol which had
fanned them since the days of his childhood; thanks
to the daily exercise with heavy barrels and with the
wagons of his peasant guests, his muscles had been well
developed. He had escaped military service and thus the
immediate dangers of the war by virtue of a trifling
physical defect—a thin white film obscured his left eye.
Upon his bare forearms, under the rolled-up shirt-
sleeves, grew forests of thick black hair. There was
something savage about his whole appearance, and his
extinguished eye could sometimes make his brown-
bearded face look even sinister. He was by nature fear-
less. Yet dread had now entered his heart to stay.

Gradually, as he made his preparations, he was able
to reassure himself somewhat, and suppress his fear of
the unknown Tarabas. Yes, he even forced himself to
get used to the idea that he himself might fall a victim
to the cruelty of this man of iron from afar. And if he
was now to suffer a dreadful end, thought Kristian-

poller, at least it would be a brave one, too. And he
looked at the iron bar which he had fetched out of the
cellar and propped against the bar. The dampness of
the cellar had rusted it a little. The brown stains reminded one of blood long dried.

It was the hour of the midday meal, and Kristianpoller received the officers living in his house, who now
entered the parlour with much shouting and jingling
of metal. He hated them. For four years now, his smiling face hiding the alternate fury and terror of his
heart, he had endured the sight of the various uniforms,
the sound of various kinds of clattering swords, of the
dull thud of carbine and rifle butts upon the wooden
floor of his parlour, the clink of spurs and the brutal
tramp of riding-boots, the creak of leather in which
the pistols hung and the clatter of mess-bowls knocking
against field-flasks. Kristianpoller had hoped that, once
the war was over, he would see another kind of cus-
tomer again, the peasants from the villages, tradesmen
from other towns, shy and cunning Jews with contra-
band brandy for sale. But the fashion for war was not,
apparently, a passing one. They were even inventing
brand-new regimentals and insignia of an even later
pattern. Kristianpoller could no longer recognize with
certainty his new guests' rank. For safety's sake he
called each one "Colonel." And he had made up his
mind to address Tarabas as "General" and "Your
Excellency."

He came round the bar smiling and bowing without intermission, and secretly wishing each of them without exception an agonizing death. They gorged and drank, but since this new land had risen into being they had not paid. They got no pay themselves, consequently they had no money. The Jew Kristianpoller regarded the finances of his new country with grave misgiving. These gentlemen were certainly waiting for Tarabas, and for the new regiment. They talked of him incessantly, and Kristianpoller's sharp and clever ears let little escape them whilst he waited upon his guests. The Jew did not venture to ask them any questions on his own account. Undoubtedly they could have told him much. They all knew him.

All at once, in the middle of the meal, the door was thrown violently open. One of Tarabas's armed guards entered, saluted with a click of heels, and remained standing at the door, a statue fearful to behold. "Tarabas's messenger," said the inn-keeper to himself. "Soon he will be here himself."

And indeed a moment later the clanking footsteps of soldiers could be heard approaching. Through the opened door strode Colonel Tarabas, followed by his bodyguard. The door remained open. All the officers leapt to their feet. Colonel Tarabas saluted and motioned them to sit down again. He turned to the Jew Kristianpoller, who had stood the whole time in an obsequious attitude in front of his counter, and ordered

food, drink, and accommodation for twelve without
delay. He, too, would put up here, said Tarabas. He
wanted a room that you could move about in. A bed
outside the door for his servant. He wished to have
twelve of his men in his immediate neighbourhood.
What he expected of the inn-keeper and whatever servants there might be was punctuality, cleanliness, and
obedience. And he concluded with this: "Repeat what
I've just said, Jew!"

Word for word each wish of Colonel Tarabas's was
repeated by Kristianpoller. The repetition was an easy
enough task. For the words of Tarabas had buried
themselves in Kristianpoller's brain like nails driven
into wax. And there they would stay imbedded till the
end of time. He said them back now word for word,
his face still bent towards the ground, his eyes upon
the shining toe-caps of Tarabas's boots and on the silver rim which the mud had left round the soles. He
might make me clean the edge of his soles with my
tongue, thought Kristianpoller. Woe is me if he should!

"Look me in the face, Jew!" said Tarabas.

Kristianpoller stood upright.

"Where's your answer?" demanded Tarabas.

"Your Excellency," answered Kristianpoller, "everything is in readiness. A large room is at Your Excellency's disposal. Your Excellency's escort will be put
up comfortably. And we will make up a bed outside
Your Excellency's door, a good bed."

"Very good, very good," said Tarabas. And he sent his men to get food from the kitchen. He sat down at an unoccupied table. There was silence in the room. The officers did not stir. They talked no more. Their forks and spoons lay untouched beside their plates.

"Good appetite!" cried Tarabas, pulling his knife out of his boot. He inspected it carefully, licked his thumb, and passed it gently across the blade.

The Jew Kristianpoller approached with a steaming bowl in his right hand, spoon and fork in his left. He had brought a dish of peas and sauerkraut with a pinkly gleaming rib of pork in it. The whole was veiled in a soft grey cloud of steam. When Kristianpoller had put down the bowl, he bowed and retreated backwards to the bar.

From behind the counter he observed between half-shut eyelids the extremely healthy appetite of the terrible Tarabas. He did not dare, not having been called upon to do so, to obey the prompting of the inner voice which told him to offer the mighty one strong drink. No, he would wait for the command to come.

"Something to drink!" the terrible one cried at last.

Kristianpoller vanished and reappeared a moment later with three large bottles on a stout wooden tray—wine, beer, spirits. He put the three bottles together with three separate glasses on the table before Tarabas and withdrew once more, bowing deeply. Tarabas first tested the bottles, raising each one in turn and examin-

ing it in the air as if to put it to the proof of hand and
eye. Finally he decided in favour of the brandy. True to
the habit of all drinkers of hard liquor, he emptied one
glass at a single draught, and poured out another.
There was still complete silence in the room. The officers sat stiffly with their plates and glasses in front of
them and looked furtively across them at the colonel.
Kristianpoller stood immobile and head down before
his counter, waiting and alert to hasten over at a gesture, yes, at a flicker of an eyelash from Colonel Tarabas. He stood there intent upon the wishes of the
war-god of Koropta, ready to spring to meet them as
they formed slowly, or—who knew?—perhaps with
suddenness within that mind. The gurgling of the
brandy as the colonel poured out another glassful could
be heard distinctly all over the large room. It was followed by the terrible one's praise: "Good stuff, this,
Jew!"—a phrase which Tarabas now began to reiterate
with shorter and shorter pauses between, and each time
in a louder voice. At last, when the colonel had disposed of his sixth glass, the youngest of the officers
present, Lieutenant Kulin, thought that the time had
come to break the silence which respect and fear had
until then imposed on all of them. He rose, a glass of
brandy in his hand, and went across to the colonel's
table. The lieutenant's hand was steady; not a drop
overflowed from the brimming glass he held. He
stopped at the table and drew himself up smartly.

"To the health of our first colonel!" said Lieutenant Kulin.

All the officers rose.

"Long live the new army!" said Tarabas.

"Long live the new army!" they rejoined.

And amidst the clink of glasses meeting one another in the toast, came a somewhat belated, timid echo in the voice of the Jew Kristianpoller: "Long live our new army!"

Instantly, no sooner were the words out of his mouth, than Nathan Kristianpoller was mightily afraid. And he hastened behind the bar, pushed open the little wooden door which led into the yard, called to the servant Fedya, and ordered him to fetch two barrels of spirits from the cellar. Meanwhile, in the parlour a general fraternizing was taking place. First singly, then in small groups, the men left their places and, with rapidly increasing courage and confidence, approached the colonel's table, where each one separately drank his health. Tarabas felt increasingly happy and at home. Still more than the spirits, the respectful friendship of the officers warmed him; vanity warmed his heart.

"Listen, my dear chap," he was soon saying indiscriminately to this and that one.

And soon the tables were pushed together. Panting and with perspiring faces Kristianpoller and Fedya came with the brandy kegs. A while later the white and fiery fluid was pouring into roomy, gleaming wine-

glasses, thirty-six in number, waiting on the bar counter. The moment one was filled, it passed from hand
to hand like a bucket at a fire. As though they were a
company of firemen, the officers lined up in a chain
from Kristianpoller's counter to the table at which the
terrible Tarabas sat, handing the fresh-filled glasses
to each other. One after another was handed down the
row—and they were of goodly size.

At a sign from Major Kulubeitis, they raised their
glasses all together and roared out an unearthly "Hur-
rah!" which quite undid the Jew Kristianpoller, but
rejoiced the servant Fedya so much that he burst out
into a peal of laughter. He laughed so hard that he
could not stand up straight, it shook him so. And he
beat his plump thighs with his clumsy hands. This
foolish laughter, so far from offending the gentlemen,
as Kristianpoller had begun to fear, did the reverse;
the good-humoured officers caught its contagion, and
now everyone laughed with Fedya, touched glasses,
guffawed, shook, roared and coughed with merriment.
Suddenly a merciless hilarity had them in its toils; they
were bound and delivered, given up to their own laughter. Yes, and Tarabas, the man of might, amidst the
wild unabating gaiety, beckoned the laughing Fedya
to him and ordered him to dance. And so that music
might not be lacking, Tarabas had one of his men
called in, one Kaleyczuk, an admirable manipulator of
the accordion. He took up his position with his chest

well out and his instrument across it, and began to play. He struck up the celebrated Cossack dance, for he had immediately recognized a brother-Cossack in Fedya. And at once, caught heart and feet by the music of the accordion, Fedya danced. The chain formed by the officers closed now into a ring, in the centre of which Fedya hopped and Kaleyczuk accompanied him with a will. Willingly, even blissfully, Fedya had embarked upon the dance. But gradually, under the spell of the music, which imposed its will upon him and which he yielded to with a submission at once sweet and agonizing, gradually the smile froze upon his face and his open mouth refused to shut. Between his yellow teeth his tongue showed now and then, moving thirstily as though to lick the air the lungs were panting for in vain. He revolved on his own axis, then dropped and twirled round squatting, and rose again to perform a leap into the air, all as the rules of the Cossack dance prescribed. It was clear to see that he would have gladly stopped. Sometimes it seemed as though all the dancer's strength was going out of him, had gone already, and that only the ardent, melancholy music still drove and animated him, and the rhythmic beat of the officers' clapping hands, as they stood around him, drawn up like guardians of the rite.

Soon the musician Kaleyczuk himself was seized with a desire to set his feet in motion. His own music overwhelmed him so completely that, his agile fingers still uninterruptedly pressing the accordion keys, he too suddenly began to turn, to hop, to squat and dance towards the indefatigable Fedya. And lastly some of the officers left the circle and vied with the two dancers as best they could, whilst the others unceasingly pounded out the measure with their heavily booted feet and with their clapping hands.

A monstrous noise arose. The floor resounded with the stamping, the window-panes clattered, the spurs clanked, and the empty glasses too, which stood side by side upon the tin-covered counter and seemed to wait for drinkers yet to come. The Jew Kristianpoller did not dare to move from the spot where he was standing. Strangely enough the din calmed him in the same way that it frightened him. But he was in dread lest they should suddenly take it into their heads to make him dance like the servant Fedya. Hatred was in his heart, and apprehension. He found himself wishing that these men might go on drinking, although he very well knew that they had no money to pay for what they took. Motionless he stood beside his counter, a stranger in his own house. And what to do he knew not. And he wanted to leave his place and go away— and knew that this also was out of the question. All at a loss, miserable and busy despite his outward immobility, he stood there, the Jew Kristianpoller.

Meanwhile the golden autumn day was drawing to its close. And upon the rack opposite the window, on

which the tanned and greasy leather belts and glittering swords were hung, the red sunset was mirrored.
Upon this sun as it went down the Jew Kristianpoller
fixed his eyes. It seemed to him a sign and token that
the ancient God existed still. He knew, the Jew, that
the sun went down in the west, and that on every
cloudless day it shone upon that rack, yet in that moment he drew solace from the most everyday, the most
familiar things. What if this Tarabas were come, this
terrible one? God's sun still went down to its setting
as on every other day. It was the hour of the evening
prayer, said with the face turned towards the east;
towards the rack, then, which he was already looking
at. How could he pray? The noise grew louder and
louder. All the terrors of the war and of the previous
changing occupations of the town since then, seemed
at that moment to Kristianpoller harmless in compari-
son with the quite undangerous roaring and stamping
of the men round Tarabas.

As for Tarabas himself, he alone had not left his
table. He sat leaning far back, rather lying than sitting,
his legs in the skin-tight trousers spread wide, his feet
in the immaculate boots stretched out far in front of
him. From time to time he felt it incumbent upon him
to clap his hands, as the others were doing ceaselessly.
A good dozen empty glasses stood now upon his table,
and were joined continuously by another and another
full one, brought like a ritual offering by the attentive

hands of the officers in the circle. Except for Tarabas
no one had drunk anything for half an hour. From his
counter the Jew Kristianpoller could see when it was
time for him to fill another glass. Indeed his eyes were
riveted upon the table of Colonel Tarabas, and neither
the din, which almost deafened him, nor the manifold
anxieties which filled him could distract his mind from
the supreme care of the moment—whether the frightful one was ready for something more to drink. Tarabas
now ignored the bottle which Kristianpoller had set
down on his table. Obviously he preferred to let the
officers wait upon him. And now, or so it seemed to
Kristianpoller, tiredness began to overcome him. At the
host's rough guess he must have accounted for some
sixteen glasses. He yawned, the great man; Kristianpoller distinctly saw him do it. And this unequivocal
expression of a universal human weakness reassured
the Jew.

Meanwhile the bright reflection of the evening sun
was quickly disappearing from the hotel parlour. It
grew dark, almost in a moment. Suddenly there was
the sound of a heavy fall. Fedya lay outstretched on
his back with his arms flung out, and the accordion
broke off as though someone had cut it in two. Someone shouted: "Water!" Kristianpoller rushed up with a
pail which always stood in readiness behind the bar,
and dashed a cold and heavy swath into Fedya's face.
The surrounding audience observed with great exacti-

tude and with more interest than alarm how Fedya emerged from his faint, guffawed, and on the instant of his return to life, still lying where he had fallen, went off again into another roar of laughter . . . just as a new-born child greets the light of day with a woeful crying.

By this time it had grown completely dark. "Light up!" cried Tarabas, and rose. Kristianpoller first lit the lantern which always stood upon the counter; he held a paper spill to its flame and lit the oil lamp with this, as he did on every evening of his life. The murky, yellow shine fell upon Fedya, who, still laughing, was scrambling to his feet. He puffed and blew; the water poured off his head and shoulders. The others were all silent. No one moved.

"How much?" cried Tarabas suddenly. How long it was since the Jew Kristianpoller had heard that call! Who had ever shouted "How much?"

"Your Excellency, General," said Kristianpoller, "I beg your pardon, but I haven't been keeping count. . . ."

"From tomorrow on you'll keep count!" said Tarabas. "How about a walk, gentlemen?"

And all made haste to gird themselves and go. With racket and clatter they left the inn and passed into the darkness of the little town of Koropta, with Tarabas heading the pack. Their destination was the barracks, to see how the new regiment was conducting itself in the darkness.

11

IN the days that followed, Colonel Tarabas, the terrible king of Koropta, ceased to feel at home within his kingdom. When he awoke in the morning in the wide and cosy bed which Kristianpoller had destined for his comfort, King Tarabas no longer knew what had taken place the day before. And the expectation of that which the day itself might bring only added to the confusion in his mind. For the events accumulating round the colonel day by day were truly such as to bewilder him; the devil was in them. Devilish papers were delivered to him by frequent couriers hot-foot from the capital, some in carriages, some on horse-back, some in ancient army motor-cars, some on foot. Tarabas had no doubt whatever that his new country was under the rule of a paper devil, at whose direction thousands of rabid clerks in the new capital sat concocting ruseful plans for the undoing of Tarabas. Red-haired clerks they were, red-haired Jews perhaps.

Every morning the colonel's orderly had to dress, shave, and brush down his master. He must put on the tight and heavy riding-boots, kneel down beside the bed, bend forward his head and shoulders between the

colonel's outspread legs and then bend back again, his
strong brown hands alternately working at the pulling-
straps of either boot, after which he must crouch back
and pound the heels and soles energetically until the
feet were settled comfortably in their encasement. For
it was as though all Tarabas's repugnance for the new
day which stood and threatened him outside the window collected into his rebellious feet. To force them to
accept the earth again he then would stamp a few times
violently where he stood, and stretch himself, yawning
with a hollow, long-drawn howl. Lastly he allowed
himself to be belted and armed with pistol and dagger
at his sides. It looked like the harnessing of a royal
steed. This was the moment when the Jew Kristianpoller, having eavesdropped at the door since earliest
dawn, hurried on silent slippers down into the bar to
make the tea. When the colonel at length emerged
into the parlour, Kristianpoller called out a "good-
morning" that sounded as though it was meant to greet
a whole town with. The Jew's great joy at finally seeing his illustrious guest again seemed to ring out in
the resounding welcome.

"Good morning, Jew," answered the terrible one.

Kristianpoller's noisy greeting was pleasant to his
ear; it made him feel properly awake at last, and gave
him the confirmation that he was still mightier than
the approaching day, no matter what new quantities
of paper it might bring. Greedily and in huge gulps

he drank the boiling tea, then left the table, saluted, and went his rattling way to the barracks. Everyone made way for him along the route, and stood still, bowing low, until he passed. But he looked at nobody.

Fresh misfortune awaited him in his office. He was an educated man, a university man even. At one time, years ago, he had been able to understand the most confounded formulæ; he had passed examinations. Ah, he had had a pretty good head on his shoulders, had Tarabas! Today he had appointed two captains to help him; four clerks in charge of a non-commissioned officer experienced in that line of work sat there and wrote—like devils too. All of these people together made still further complications of the innumerable decrees arriving from the capital; they solved none of the many enigmas, but only thickened the fog which seemed to rise out of the papers. They appeared before Tarabas with unintelligible reports, asked him if they should do this and that, and when he told them kindly to leave him in peace they vanished like ghosts, the earth swallowed them up, and there he was, left alone with all the torment of responsibility! Ah, he longed for war, the mighty Tarabas! The random horde which composed this new army of his were not his soldiers of the old days. Hunger had driven them to Tarabas, nothing else. Every day new desertions were reported. Every day he came into the drill ground he noticed fresh gaps in the lines. The drilling was slatternly and

no more than half awake. Yes, some of his officers had
not a notion even how to drill a company. What a horror for a Tarabas! He could rely on no one but the
few faithful men of his old guard whom he had
brought there with him to this Koropta. The others
feared him still, that was certain; but already he had
begun to feel that that fear might bring forth treach-
ery and even assassination. Were his commands still
carried out? They were merely received without demur.
Resistance would have pleased him better. And Tarabas called back to mind the fatal Sunday when the red
stranger had appeared before him for the first time,
and the great havoc had begun. Now and then a bitter
hatred of his subordinates overwhelmed him, as it
never had against the enemy. And in the evenings when
he was sure that all these enemies were long since
asleep, he would get up from the peaceful table in the
inn, leave his drinking comrades without a greeting,
and hurry off to the barracks, striding fiercely and
thirsting for revenge. He inspected the guard, left the
dormitories open, pulled the covers from the sleepers'
naked bodies, searched beds and straw mattresses, ruck-
sacks and bundles, pockets and pillows, even the water-
closets, threatened to shoot all and sundry, demanded
to see their military papers and passports, questioned
this one and that as to the battles he had fought in,
was suddenly touched and within a hair's breadth of
apologizing, then filled again with new fury, this time

88

against himself, followed by pity and sadness. Profoundly ashamed, but hiding the shame behind his clattering frightfulness, he would depart stamping—how gladly would he have made his steps inaudible—and return to the inn.

So far no pay had been sent him for his men, nor for himself and his officers either. His old guard stole and pilfered what they required, in houses and farmyards, as they had always done. In accordance with the custom prevailing in conquered territory, he had ordered the inhabitants to deliver foodstuffs to the regiment every afternoon until further orders. Every day on the stroke of four o'clock the townsfolk of Koropta stood in the barracks yard with bundles and baskets. For the meat, eggs, butter, and cheese they brought they received so-called receipts, tiny scraps of paper, bits of discoloured waste stationery from the offices, written on in Kontsev's unschooled hand and signed by Tarabas with an energetic "T." One day, according to Tarabas's announcement, proclaimed with a loud flourish of drums by three of his own men in the streets of Koropta, these receipts would be honoured and paid out against in cash. But the people did not believe the drummers. How often in the course of this war had drummers said the same to the Koropta folk! But frightened now, as then, they brought what they could spare to the barracks, either from their own stores or else bought for the purpose—and even the

poorest contributed their mite, a pot of dripping, a slice
of bread, potatoes, turnips, radishes, or baked apples.

The Jew Kristianpoller boarded the insatiable officers. The ancient, helpful, cruel God sent to the Jew
Kristianpoller each new day a new gift. From the ham-
let of Hupki came his good brother-in-law, Leib, with
half an ox. And on the next day the slaughterer Kuropkin put in an unlooked-for appearance, hoping to exchange a stolen pig for a quart of brandy. He had not
hoped in vain. Two quarts Kristianpoller gave him for
it. For this Kuropkin slew the pig with his own hands
and roasted it on a fire in the open yard. With money
only the terrible Tarabas had paid so far; from the
others Kristianpoller had not had even receipts. But
what was the use of this new money which the new
state was circulating, these hastily printed paper notes?
Would they ever be exchanged for honest cash in Kristianpoller's lifetime? Hard gold, five rolls of ten-ruble
pieces, each a yard high—Kristianpoller had them
stored in the second subterranean story of his cellar.
He was envisaging the time when, if he must go on
satisfying the greed of his hated guests, he would have
to go down there and take something away from one
of the rolls. But he prayed that that time might not
come by many a long day yet.

Tarabas had already sent word to the capital that
money was needed, and that, if it did not come soon,
unrest and mutiny might be expected. A very few days

after this an elegant lieutenant in the new uniform of the country appeared in Koropta, just at the hour when Colonel Tarabas was in the habit of spending a convivial hour with his brother-officers. The lieutenant announced that on the following day His Excellency, General Lakubeit, would inspect the garrison. Tarabas rose.

"Is the general bringing money?" he asked.

"Certainly, sir!" answered the lieutenant.

"Sit down and have a drink!" commanded Tarabas.

The lieutenant obediently sat down. He drank very little. He was the adjutant of an abstinent general.

12

THE next morning General Lakubeit arrived. Tarabas received him at the station. The sight of the general, a small and weakly man, was a surprise to Tarabas; the general's diminutive stature seemed somehow deliberately designed to put Tarabas at a disadvantage. Something about His Excellency's feeble frame seemed to bode ill for Tarabas's robust one. From the step of the train the general was holding out his hand. But it seemed as though he did so for the support of Tarabas's mighty grip in alighting rather than in cordial greeting. For a moment Tarabas felt the brittle, dried-up hand in his huge palm, like a little warm and helpless bird. The colonel had counted on meeting a general like the many others he had known, powerful and masculine figures for the most part, bearded, at the least mustachioed, men with direct and soldierly eyes, hard hands and a firm walk. This was the kind of general Tarabas had prepared himself to meet. Lakubeit, however, was by all odds one of the strangest generals in the world. His clean-shaven, sallow, wizened little face grew like some strange old shrivelled fruit out of the high scarlet collar, and hid itself in the shadow of the immense black roof formed by the peak of the grey, gold-braided cap, which seemed to have been equipped with it for no other reason than to shelter the little aged head from withering further. The thin legs vanished into tall riding-boots which hardly differed from the kind the peasants wore, and had no spurs. A loose jacket flapped around His Excellency's scraggy torso. This was a scarecrow, never a general. . . .

Tarabas took so wretched an appearance as this for a piece of the most subtle malice. He liked his own kind. He loved men in his own likeness. Deep down, in his heart's secret depths, there lurked a presentiment, asleep still but muttering and warning sometimes in that sleep, that there would come a day when the mighty Tarabas would have a decisive, a fateful meeting with one of the many puny ones who go up and down upon the earth, superfluous and sly, and useless for all decent purposes. As he stepped to the general's side to accompany him towards the exit, he noticed that Lakubeit was but elbow-high to him. Discipline and courtesy impelled Colonel Tarabas to do what he could, therefore, to diminish himself by bending his back, curtailing his long stride, lowering his voice. His spurs jingled. But the general's boots made no sound.

"My dear fellow," said the general in a very gentle voice. Tarabas bent his back still lower to hear better.

"My dear fellow," said General Lakubeit, "I thank you for this kind welcome. I know a lot about you. I've known you by name a long time. I'm delighted to meet you, you know." Was this the way for a general to speak? Tarabas had no suitable answer ready.

On the way from the station, side by side in the carriage—Kristianpoller's carriage driven by one of Tarabas's own men—General Lakubeit said nothing at all. Huddled up like a very small child, he sat there beside Tarabas and let his clear, dark eyes dart with their swift glance over the view. You saw them when he took off his big, gold-braided cap, which he did a few times during the drive, although the day was anything but hot. Once or twice Tarabas tried to set a conversation going. But, hardly begun, it seemed to him as though the general had drawn miles and miles away from him. Forebodings of evil crossed the heart of the mighty Tarabas, dark forebodings! When they came into the little town where the inhabitants, well trained in servility, were lined up on the wooden sidewalks right and left to hail the great visitor, General Lakubeit began to turn from side to side and smile at them as he returned their greeting, nodding his yellowish, bald head at them; he held his cap on his knees. The thin lips parted and revealed a toothless mouth. If Tarabas had doubted before, he was certain now—the topmost of all the havoc-wreaking paper devils was this one, Lakubeit.

At Kristianpoller's place they stopped; the general jumped out nimbly, paying no attention to Tarabas.

He nodded pleasantly at the inn-keeper, made haste to replace his cap upon his little head, and fairly darted into the house. He ordered tea and a hard-boiled egg. And Tarabas did not touch the glass of brandy which Kristianpoller had placed before him as usual without waiting to be told. The general was knocking the egg gently against the edge of his saucer as the elegant lieutenant, his adjutant, entered and drew himself up smartly beside the table.

"Sit down," murmured the general, and peeled the egg clean with his bony first finger.

When the egg had been eaten and the tea drunk in utter silence, General Lakubeit said: "Now we'll go and have a look at the regiment!"

By all means, Colonel Tarabas had seen to everything. Since early morning the regiment had been waiting outside the barracks for the general to arrive. And inside also everything was in the best of order. Notwithstanding Colonel Tarabas said:

"I can't guarantee that you'll find it much to look at. I'd no pay for the men, no uniforms; even the barracks were uninhabitable when I got here. Nor can I answer for all the men. A lot of them have deserted. There's a good deal of riff-raff among them, I'm afraid."

"Have your drink first," said the general.

Tarabas had it.

"You have one too," said the general to the lieutenant.

"Two chests of money will be here later on today," he went on. "That ought to settle the chief difficulties. You'll have officers' and men's pay for two months. Also something over for beer and spirits. Good humour's the principal thing. You know that, don't you, Colonel Tarabas?"

Yes, Colonel Tarabas knew that.

In silence they re-entered the carriage and bowled along to the barracks.

With hasty little steps General Lakubeit pattered past the ranks drawn up on parade. He took his cap off often; it seemed to be a habit of his. Without it, bareheaded, his nude little skull was just level with the shouldered rifle-butts, and one could not but think that his quick eyes took in nothing but the belts and boots of the regiment he was reviewing. The men performed the usual head-turns, but their eyes looked out in front of them, far above Lakubeit's head. But now and then, with startling suddenness, his head came up, he stopped, his swift eyes set hard and bored into the face, the body, the harness of a man or officer at random.

Unlike all other generals in the world, General Lakubeit did not seem to judge the military qualities of the men he inspected. They were well used to being tested on that score. They were versed in war and in imprisonment, in giving battle and receiving wounds, even in dying—what fault had the general to find with them?

This tiny Lakubeit, however, when he stopped and jerked his head up with such suddenness, seemed trying to probe the soul, the inmost, of a man. They, to conceal this from him, armoured themselves with military stiffness, wrapped themselves round in discipline, stood absolutely rigid as in their earliest recruiting days, and with it all the feeling still tormented them that it was waste of effort. Most of them believed in the existence of the devil. And, like their colonel, they too believed that they could see the little flames of hell flickering in Lakubeit's small eyes.

Lakubeit brought the review very quickly to an end. He went into the office with Colonel Tarabas, gave orders for the clerks to be sent away, sat down, glanced through the papers, arranged them with his skilful, skinny hands in separate piles, smiled occasionally, smoothed one pile tenderly and then another, looked at Tarabas sitting opposite him, and said:

"Colonel Tarabas, you don't understand all this!"

So there was something, apparently, which the mighty Tarabas did not understand; though everybody knows that, since Tarabas had gone into the war, such a thing did not exist.

"Yes," General Lakubeit repeated in his thin voice, "you don't understand these things, Colonel Tarabas."

"No," said the mighty Tarabas, "no, I don't. I can't make head or tail of them. The two captains I put on to the work because I thought that they were experts—

they were in the statistics department during the war—
and the clerks I got down specially, they don't understand this business either. They bring me reports that
I can't make head or tail of; I admit it. I'm afraid they
only complicate things worse than ever."

"Exactly," said General Lakubeit. "I shall send you
an adjutant, Colonel Tarabas. A young fellow. Don't
treat him with too much contempt, will you? He was
not at the front. Feeble constitution. Not fit. Not one
of nature's soldiers like, thank heaven, you are, Colonel.
As a matter of fact he was my assistant for ten years
before the war. I must tell you—I hope it won't make
any difference—that I was a lawyer in my civilian days.
And an auditor in the war, not a fighting man. You'll
have noticed that, most likely. And your father's lawyer, by the way. I saw him only a week ago and had
a talk with him, your old father. He didn't send you
his love."

General Lakubeit paused. His penetrating, monotonous words seemed to stand there in the room, each
one for itself; hard, sharp, they stood still all round
Colonel Tarabas like a little fence of thin, planed posts.
Only the small word "Father" broke their uniformity,
and stood up more noticeable than the rest. All at once
Colonel Tarabas seemed to feel himself growing
smaller and smaller; yes, without doubt he felt himself undergoing a physical shrinking. Whereas earlier
in the day he had in vain endeavoured, out of polite-

ness and deference to his superior officer, to make himself appear less than the general, now he did all he could to maintain his proper size, and sit there bolt upright and broad, like the mighty Tarabas he was. He could still look through the window over the top of General Lakubeit's bald head, and noted the fact with satisfaction. Outside was sunlit autumn. A golden chestnut tree stood near the window, with half its leaves already gone. Behind it, looking near enough to touch, shone the intense blue of the sky. For the first time since his childhood Colonel Tarabas was conscious of the strength and power of nature; he could smell the autumn through the window, and wished that he might be a boy again. For a short while he sank into a reverie of his childhood, but knew as well that he was only taking flight there from this present hour, that he was only running away from it back into the past, the mighty Tarabas. Whereat he went on growing small, infinitesimal, until at last he sat there before General Lakubeit like a little boy.

"I've been meaning to go and see my people," he lied.

General Lakubeit seemed not to hear this remark.

"I knew you," said Lakubeit, "when you were still a lad. I've often visited your father. And then you were mixed up in that St. Petersburg affair. You recollect. It cost enormous trouble—and money, an enormous lot of money too. After that you went to America. Then there was the episode with that bar-keeper you had a fight with. . . ."

"The bar-keeper?" said Tarabas.

How long it was since he had thought about that man, and about Katharina. Now he saw them all again, Katharina, the café-owner's immense red maw, his cousin Maria, the heavy silver cross between her breasts, the large glass globe and the gipsy's face beyond it.

"In New York," Tarabas began suddenly, and it was as though somebody else were telling it, some other speaking through his mouth, "at an amusement park in New York a gipsy told my fortune; she said that I would be a murderer and a saint. . . . I believe the first part of that prophecy . . ."

"Colonel Tarabas," said little Lakubeit, holding his thin claw up to his face with the fingers far apart, "the first part of that prophecy has not yet been fulfilled. You did not kill that man in New York. He's not alive, however. He joined up in the war and was killed. At Ypres, to be exact. That affair gave us a lot of trouble, too. Justice, you know—if you'll allow me to digress a moment—does not let wars interfere with it. You were kept track of. There would have been a nice degradation in store for you if you had done for the good man that time. And by the by, the young man I'm sending down here to you looked after that matter for you. You've something to thank him for, I assure you! Your father was in a state!"

It was very quiet. Lakubeit's monotonous voice moved like a breeze, a gentle one, blowing towards Colonel Tarabas. A gentle, stubborn, inescapable breeze. It, too, was wholly familiar, and disagreeable at the same time. It rose out of wholly familiar, disagreeable, long-forgotten years.

"And my cousin Maria?" asked Tarabas.

"She is married," said Lakubeit. "She's married to a German officer. It seems she fell in love with him."

"I was in love with her too," said Tarabas.

There was no sound after that. Lakubeit folded his hands. His fingers thrust through each other made a bony fence across the table with the neat piles of documents behind it.

But Colonel Tarabas let his hands lie limp and loose upon his thighs. He felt that he could lift neither his hands from his legs nor his feet from the floor. Maria had fallen in love with a foreign officer. The mighty Tarabas had been betrayed! Another had wronged the terrible Tarabas, who until then had only wronged and done violence to others. Poor Tarabas was the victim of great and bitter wrong. It mitigated somewhat his own violence; it was, therefore, when all is said and done, a kindly wrong. It is atonement, atonement, O Tarabas, thou man of violence!

"The chief thing," General Lakubeit began, "the chief thing is for you to clean up this regiment of yours. You'll have to throw out at least half of them. We

shall require precise information as to the origins of
every single one you keep. Colonel Tarabas, we're
building up a new army. It must be an army we can
rely upon. The men from here, there, and everywhere
that you can't keep, we'll deport them or lock them
up, or hand them over to their various consuls. In short,
we'll get rid of them by some means or other. It
doesn't matter really how. Be sure and keep enough
musicians. Music is important. And—all else being
equal—keep as many as you can that can read and
write. But give them all their full pay. Those you're
getting rid of, too. You'll find it easier to get them to
give up their arms if you see that they have plenty of
beer tomorrow and the day after. Say it's the general's
treat, if you like.—Well, that's all, I think!" concluded
Lakubeit, and rose.

In silence, as they had come, they drove to the station. It was evening. The station lay past Koropta to
the west. The highroad went straight as an arrow towards the setting sun, which, seen above the yellow
brick of the station, showed a sad flushed face beyond
the smoke-clouds of the shunting engines. Its reflection
hung in the immense and shiny black peak of the
general's cap. The elegant lieutenant on the back seat
stared, stiff and silent, at this small reflection.

"Good luck!" said General Lakubeit, about to board
the train. His dried-up little hand was strangely warm,
a helpless bird in the mighty grip of mighty Tarabas.

"Don't forget the beer, and if you think the situation calls for vodka, let them have it," Lakubeit added from the carriage window.

The train steamed out—and the mighty Tarabas was alone; alone, it seemed to him, as he had never been in all his life before.

13

THEREFORE he drank, on that disastrous day, far more than usual. He drank so much that the Jew Kristianpoller began to cast round in his mind for a means whereby he might dilute the spirits with a little water. Life had ceased to smile upon Kristianpoller, although he already knew that two chests of money for the officers and men had arrived late that afternoon. Two non-commissioned officers and six privates, all with carbines in their hands, had escorted the automobile. It was still standing in Kristianpoller's yard. The chests were inside. A sentinel marched up and down outside the door. It was he who prevented the Jew from diluting the brandy.

Above the entrance to the out-house a lantern swung gently in the evening wind, shedding an oily, yellow gleam over the yard. One could hear from the parlour the sentinel's measured, hob-nailed footsteps, and this although the officers were gathered at their tables in full force, as usual. But they did not talk, they whispered. For in their midst, as though upon an island of silence, immured within a wall of mute, transparent

ice, sat Colonel Tarabas, alone at his own table. He
was drinking.

The whole world had deserted Tarabas. It had forgotten him and spat him out. The war was over. Even
the war had deserted him. There was no danger left
to hope for. Tarabas felt betrayed by the peace. He
could not understand this business of the regiment. His
cousin Maria had betrayed him. His father and mother
had not sent him their love. They betrayed him too.
Forgotten, deserted, spat out and betrayed, was Colonel
Tarabas.

The regiment that he had got together was good for
nothing. He was aware of it himself. Tomorrow he
would have to send half of them away—disarm and
turn them off. He rose, already not quite steady on his
feet. He went into the yard to his own men that he
could trust.

He called for Kontsev, his oldest sergeant-major.
Kontsev had been serving under Tarabas for three
years now, and more.

"My dear fellow," said Tarabas. "My dear fellow,"
Tarabas repeated; he was not quite clear in his speech.

The huge form of Sergeant-Major Kontsev merged
under the starry dome of the clear night, wanly lit by
the yellow-gleaming lantern, and stood immobile before the colonel. "Come with me," said Tarabas. And
the colossus Kontsev set himself in motion. Seeing that
Tarabas stumbled a little, he walked stooping, thus

offering the colonel his shoulder for support. Tarabas flung his arm round Kontsev's shoulder. He tried to bring the great bearded face close to his own; the smell of Kontsev's moustache was pleasant to him, and the tobacco- and alcohol-laden breath, oh, the whole familiar odour of the proper soldier—the dampness which the woolly stuff of the uniform exuded, the earthiness of the heavy, cloddish hands, the leathernness of boots and straps. These scents could move Colonel Tarabas to tears. Already two scalding drops were stealing down his cheeks. Tarabas could not speak. He staggered, embracing with one arm the stooping, shortened giant Kontsev, into the farthest, darkest corner of the yard.

"Kontsev," Tarabas began, and it was the first time he had talked so to his sergeant-major, "my dear old Kontsev, our regiment's no good. The general told me so today, but we two knew it without that, didn't we, my Kontsev? My good old Kontsev, there's nothing to be done about it, we'll have to let the bad half go tomorrow. And we must get them drunk."

"Yes, sir," Kontsev answered him. "We'll get them drunk, and we'll get rid of them all right. We'll get their guns and things away from them. And their ammunition too," he said after a while, by way of special consolation. He was a good ten years older and two inches taller than Colonel Tarabas, and his manner now was very fatherly.

"Remember the war, Kontsev," said the colonel.

"That was a grand time, wasn't it? No collecting regiments then. Just shooting, that's all—and you either got through or you kicked the bucket. Quite simple. Wasn't it, Kontsev?"

"Yes, it was," said the colossus. "The war! That was something like! We'll not have another one though, not while we're alive—never any more!"

"It was splendid!" said Tarabas.

"Glorious!" Kontsev confirmed him.

"We'll let them off the march tomorrow," said Tarabas. "We'll say the general has given them a day off for drinking. Let them begin at six in the morning. In the evening we'll get them away under escort."

"We have four lorries," Kontsev agreed. "Best go back now, sir." And once more, bent to a good inch less than nature had made him, he accompanied Colonel Tarabas back to the inn parlour.

"Let me embrace you, Kontsev," said Tarabas on the threshold. But Kontsev stepped smartly in front of him, pushed open the door, and stood immovable in the doorway until Tarabas had entered. Thereupon he saluted, and with a single giant stride was gone. For a while the tread of his mighty boots could still be heard tramping about in the dark ground of the yard.

Tarabas sat down again at his table, and there he remained, while in front of him the glasses formed up in a row like glittering soldiers on parade. Gradually the officers, one after another, left the room, each with a silent salute to the colonel. Alone at his table Tarabas sat on. Behind the counter sat the inn-keeper Kristian-poller.

It was obvious that Colonel Tarabas had no intention of getting up again that night. On the wall above the bar Kristianpoller's clock struck hour after hour. In between, one heard only its steady iron ticking, and the regular, hob-nailed footsteps of the sentinel in the yard outside. Each time Colonel Tarabas raised his glass to his lips, Kristianpoller started out of his doze and prepared to fill the next one. More sinister even than the ceaselessly drinking Tarabas seemed to him the perfect silence of this night; it weighed upon him so intolerably that he was positively glad when Tarabas moved to take up his glass and set it down again. From time to time both men glanced towards the window, at the narrow square of the starry, dark blue sky. Then their eyes would meet. And the more often their eyes encountered each other, the more intimate the two men seemed to become.

"Yes, yes, Jew, I know!" said the eyes of Colonel Tarabas. And "Yes, yes, you poor hero, I too!" said the Jew Kristianpoller's one sound eye.

14

DAY broke. A fine day. It rose with gentle indifference out of soft mists. Kristianpoller was the first to wake. He had fallen asleep behind his counter; he could not remember at what hour. Colonel Tarabas was with him still. He was asleep. He was snoring powerfully, his head upon his folded arms sprawled across the table, with the glittering empty glasses now a disorderly rout in front of him. The colonel's broad, now slightly stooping back rose and fell with the heavy breaths he drew. Kristianpoller contemplated the sleeping Tarabas, wondering whether he should dare to take it upon himself to wake him. The clock above the counter said half-past eight. Kristianpoller remembered the tired, gentle, kindly expression which had shone out of the drunken eyes of Colonel Tarabas in the small hours of that night, and crossed resolutely to the table. He touched the shoulder of the terrible one with a timid finger. Tarabas jumped up at once, cheerful, even gay. His sleep had been short, uncomfortable, and very deep. He felt strong. He was in excellent spirits. He ordered tea. He shouted for his orderly, stretched out his legs to have his boots polished while he drank, bit into an enormous slice of bread and butter, and with his mouth still full called for a mirror, which the Jew Kristianpoller took down from the wall and brought to the table, where he stood holding it up to Tarabas.

"Shave!" cried Tarabas. And his orderly brought soap and razor, and Tarabas fitted his red nape into the hard back of the chair. While he was being shaved, he whistled cheerful tunes which he made up as he went along, slapping out the time against his great thighs. The day shone ever brighter and more golden.

"Open the window!" commanded Tarabas.

Through the open window the early but already dense blue of the autumn sky streamed into the room. The merry chatter of the sparrows filled the air as on a warm day before the spring has really come. It seemed as though there was not going to be a winter that year at all.

It was not until he came out into the yard and found his sergeant-major and five of his men already gone, that Tarabas remembered that this was a day on which unusual events were to be expected. He left the inn.

He found the single long main street of Koropta in a state of unwonted animation. In front of their little shops the Jewish shop-keepers had set out their wares on chairs and tables and wooden boxes. There were glass beads, imitation corals, fancy paper in dark-blue, gold, and silver, long scarlet sticks of sweets, cotton aprons ablaze with flowers, gleaming sickles, large pocket-knives with pink wooden handles, kerchiefs for women's heads in Turkish colours and designs. Little peasant carts moved peaceably along in single file, as though strung on a thread, all the way down the street; here and there one of their little horses neighed, and the pigs lying helpless, fastened by their hind legs in the carts and barrows, grunted into the morning, doleful and happy at the same time.

"What's all this?" asked Tarabas.

"Friday and pig-market!" answered his orderly.

"My horse!" commanded Tarabas.

Something about it all disturbed his ease. He did not like this Friday, he did not like this pig-market either. If he were to walk to the barracks as he did on other days, something untoward might easily happen on the way. He would have loved to make one sweep of the hand in passing and send the shop-keepers' whole display tumbling from the high, wooden sidewalks down into the low road, under the wheels of the peasants' little carts. He could feel a huge rage brewing in him. Friday! He would rather have ridden the whole Friday through, trampled it out of existence under his horse's hoofs. He mounted and rode among the peasant vehicles, exploding now and then with a thunderous oath when they failed to make way for him in time, sometimes spitting with sure and skilful aim at the unconscious nape of some peasant's neck moving along in front of him, sometimes tickling the terrified face of another with the thong of his leather riding-crop.

Arrived at the barracks, he saw at the first glance that his good Kontsev had done his duty. The barrels of beer and spirits which had come in on the morning train stood in two rows against the wall of the yard with five of his own men on guard beside them. It was a holiday for everyone. The officers were gathered in the shed of fresh planks which, since Tarabas's arrival there, had served as the mess. Their talkative, resounding laughter could be heard from afar. Kontsev appeared and saluted, saying nothing. It was a perfectly wordless, thoroughly eloquent report. Tarabas understood, left him standing, and went on. The men and non-commissioned officers lay or squatted about on the ground. The sun shone down upon the bare yard with ever more benevolence and warmth. Everyone was waiting in a mood of cheerfulness, contentment, and holiday.

Towards eleven o'clock they lined up for the midday meal. The tin bowls clattered in a row, the hot, thick soup out of the cauldron splashed heavily from the cook's huge ladle into them. Colonel Tarabas stood beside the field-kitchen. One after the other each man passed before him. He observed their faces closely. He was trying to discern which of these men were worth something, and which of them must be got rid of.

Yes, Tarabas hoped to know men by their faces. Vain
endeavour! But General Lakubeit could do it! To
Colonel Tarabas all their faces looked stupid, cruel,
treacherous, and sly that day. It was different in the
war. In the war one saw at once exactly what a man
was worth. None of these had red hair. None of them,
unfortunately. That would have been a certain sign.
Every red-haired man would have been eliminated by
Colonel Tarabas, and in short order.

They were in great haste to be done with eating.
Those who had spoons left them where they were inside their boots. They put the bowls to their mouths
and gulped down the thick soup, sucked the meat off
the bones, and hurled them wide over the barracks wall.
All to arrive the sooner at the promised beer. Kontsev
was the barman. Now, as the church clock began to
strike noon and the sun's heat had grown almost fierce,
innumerable drinking vessels of the most various
species appeared as if by magic; glasses, wooden, tin,
and earthenware mugs, jugs and cans, brought in bundles and armfuls post-haste by soldiers, and set down
carefully before the vats. At a gesture from Kontsev
all the taps were turned. A loud rushing and foaming
arose. And the faces of the soldiers, greedy though appeased, with the soupy traces of their dinner still in
their beards, and their lips already moving with the
water that gathered in their thirsty mouths, now lit up
with a flame of almost sacred rapture. It made them all

look alike, a regiment of brothers. In dense swarms they swept up to the barrels. A mighty drinking began. The vessels were not enough to go round, they had to be shared; their return was waited for impatiently, four, six hands to each mug held towards the richly, infinitely richly flowing taps. They drank beer. The white froth overflowed, soaked into the ground, hung in the corners of the mouths and in the moustaches of the men; their tongues came out and licked it off their beards, and the taste of it lingered on the palate, this extra gift of special grace which crowned the day of grace which was this festival. What a day!

Each with a tin jug filled to the brim with clear spirits, Kontsev and his five now began to push their way through the disorderly, surging crowd. They chose, changed their minds, picked out this one, then that one—without rhyme or reason, so it seemed to the men—and handed him a drink, then moved on with the grateful smile of the favoured one for thanks, and pursued by the inconsolable and disappointed gaze of the unfavoured. All those who had taken their great swallow of the vodka now felt their throats on fire, and must have more beer. But many a one, big and powerful as he was, fell instantly with a loud crash to the ground, struck by the white thunderbolt of the first draught. And it did not look as though he would ever rise again. Froth came out of the corners of his mouth, his lips were blue, the eyelids would not shut quite to,

but showed the bluish edge of the eyeball, the face was
distorted yet content, and filled with a cruel, stubborn
joy. The men thus felled were then lifted high by two
strong fellows and removed from the barracks. Four
big lorries waited at the gate. One was already half
full. The men had been disposed inside them carefully,
one next to the other, as one might pack a box of mon-
ster tin soldiers. And they threw a kindly pall of canvas
over the unconscious bodies.

It soon became apparent that Kontsev's carefully
thought-out arrangements had overlooked the im-
munity of some of these men's constitutions. Some
whom no beer nor spirits could affect profited by the
general disorder to make their longed-for escape. Silent
and stealthy so long as they were still within the pre-
cincts of the barracks, as soon as they were well away,
they lifted up their voices in loud and drunken song
and staggered down the by-paths to the little town
which they had not seen for a long time, and for which
they now felt seized with honest homesickness. Deep
was the grudge they nourished against the frightful
Tarabas ever since he had lured them into the barracks
and laid his harsh yoke upon them there. Only his old
guard lived a life worth living under him. And against
these their resentment was almost greater than against
the colonel. Once or twice the malcontents had tried to
organize a general flight or open mutiny. The malcontents! Who was not that—except his own men whom

Tarabas had brought with him to Koropta? Thither
they had swarmed to join the army, but no sooner
were their thirst and hunger stilled than they began to
long again for freedom, for freedom, sweet sister of
the bitter brother, hunger. Drilling for a new country
which belonged to no one knew whom was silly, childish, and tiring. But every time the caged ones had a
plan half formed it was infamously—and inexplicably
—betrayed to Sergeant-Major Kontsev. The punishment was hideous. Many of the plotters were made to
squat upon the narrow barracks wall for six hours at
a stretch, watched by two men with guns primed to
shoot, one inside and one outside the wall, with eyes
and gun-barrel trained upon the culprit. Kontsev was
past master in the art of inventing penalties and torments. With his own hands he would lash the outstretched arms of some to the rungs of a long ladder
which the wretched victims had thus to carry round
with them whilst they performed the various marching
steps, or ran. Others again, carrying their carbines and
full equipment, were made to race ten times without
stopping and with a running start up the steep bank
which had been raised at the farthest end of the barracks yard for use in shooting exercises. When these
and similar chastisements had been experienced once
or twice, there was an end of secret planning. But the
resentment stayed within the mind and grew.

Now they were free at last. The first eight who had

slipped out of the barracks were followed by others in
groups, this time without any previous arrangement.
It was as though the alcohol had sharpened the wits of
those whom it had not knocked into insensibility. And
though their bodies lost their equilibrium, their minds
grew clear and steady. It was not long—certainly before Kontsev and his men could realize how many had
escaped them—before the fugitives, thanks to the sure
instinct with which the drunkard gropes his way to
the right place, had reached the inn of Nathan Kristianpoller. They entered, in three or four groups; they
broke in. That day the gate stood open. For the first
time in a long while it was pig-market day in Koropta.
The Jew Kristianpoller gave praise to God for His
miracles. Great He was, though His ways defeated com-
prehension, very great in His inexplicable lovingkind-
ness. Indeed no human reason could tell why on this
day the pig-market should have suddenly taken place
as in the good old days, and brought such joy to Kristianpoller's heart. Yesterday not a soul so much as
dreamt of it! But there you are—if it is the will of God
that there should be a pig-market once again in Koropta, in the twinkling of an eye every peasant in the
district knows it, and even the pigs themselves know
it perhaps, who can tell?

When the first of the peasant guests, so long and
sadly missed, appeared at the White Eagle, Kristianpoller had the boy Fedya throw open both wings of

the double door, as in the bygone, happy days of years
ago, before ever the threshold of that inn had been
crossed by any armed man except the bland and
friendly policeman of the town. Yes, when the first of
the little country-folk arrived in the earliest morning,
as casually and calmly as though they had been there
the week before the same as ever, as though there had
been no war, no revolution, and no new country,
dressed in their familiar, acrid-smelling, whitish-yellow,
buttonless sheepskins belted in with dark-blue linen
girdles—when these good folk whom he had seen and
known all his life appeared once more after their long
absence, the Jew Kristianpoller forgot his sleepless
night, his fears, the officers, his guests, and even Tarabas. It seemed to him that the returning peasants were
the first sure sign that real peace had been restored at
last. Kristianpoller, in joyful, pious haste, had not yet
finished taking off his phylacteries and rolling them
together, when the first peasant customers entered the
parlour. With hurried obeisances the host now tried
to take his leave of God to whom he had just been
offering his devotions, and to include a greeting to the
peasants in the same motions. How sweet and peaceful
was the sharp odour of their sheepskin coats! How de-
lightful the grunting of the fettered pigs lying on the
straw-covered floor of the little carts outside. No doubt
about it, those were the voices of true peace, the sweet
and long-lost, now come back again. Peace had re-

turned to earth and stopped at Kristianpoller's inn to
rest a while.

And as in the old days the Jew Kristianpoller had
the portly little kegs brought from the cellar and set
out, not only in the yard, but some outside before the
open door to encourage all who came to slake a thirst
already keen enough. A great and pious gratitude filled
Kristianpoller. God, the Inscrutable, had covered the
world with war and devastation; but meantime He had
suffered hops and malt to flourish in abundance, and
out of these came beer, and beer was what the inn-
keeper must live by. And for all that so many men
had fallen in the war, yet the peasants, thirsty and
solid drinkers, increased and multiplied, themselves as
plentiful as malt and hops. Oh, divine grace! Oh, lovely
peace!

But whilst the godly Kristianpoller marvelled and
gave praise, already the disaster was afoot, the great
and bloody disaster of Koropta, and with it the dire
aberration of the mighty Nicholas Tarabas.

15

COLONEL TARABAS'S followers who had been left behind in the out-house in Kristianpoller's yard received the deserters with feigned pleasure. Immediately they sent news to Kontsev at the barracks that the drunken men had walked unawares into a fresh imprisonment. As for Colonel Tarabas, he had been sitting long together with the officers in the barracks mess, "to forget that it was Friday," and to forget the other agitations of this strange day as well. Sergeant-Major Kontsev brought him the report which he had just received, but Colonel Tarabas was no longer able to hear everything.

Meanwhile, evening was coming on, a Friday evening. And the Jews of Koropta were beginning, as usual, to make their preparations against the Sabbath. Kristianpoller likewise. As he moved about the kitchen where he had slept since the departure of his family, spreading a cloth upon the table and setting out the candlesticks, he thought about his wife and children, and a kind of hope that they might soon come home again stole back into his heart.

The pig-market was a certain sign that peace had returned, lasting peace. If those new bank-notes of the new country, with which the peasants had paid, were worth real gold like the good rubles of the past, the day's takings had been wonderful, just like the days before the war. Kristianpoller began to take the notes which lay all crumpled in his till, and order them, smooth them out and put them away in the numerous compartments of his two fat leather bags. On the rack close above his head appeared now, as it had done on every other day, the gold reflection of the autumn sun, preparing to go down to its usual serene setting.

Outside in the street and in the yard the peasants were getting ready for the journey home. They had bought kerchiefs, corals, sickles, and hats. They had drunk much and were in high good-humour. They all donned the new hats over the old ones, the handkerchiefs they wore like scarves, the money for the pigs they had sold they carried in bags of unbleached linen round their necks. They were cheerful and tired, pleased with themselves and with the well-spent day. Cocks crowed peacefully, and in the chaff that strewed the road, good-tempered hens and ducks and geese hunted for some delicacy of the fair. Even the dogs which had been let off their chains ran about among them without barking or threatening their weaker brethren with harm.

Nathan Kristianpoller opened his whole heart to the whole blessed peace of this declining earthly Friday

which seemed to yearn towards the divine and holy
Sabbath. Tomorrow evening, he thought, he would
write a letter to his wife in Kyrbitki, and tell her he
would like her to come home. "My darling wife," he
would say, "with the help of God we are now delivered from the war, and peace has been given back
to us. Unfortunately we still have soldiers billeted on
us, but the colonel is not as dangerous as he looks;
in fact, when one thinks what a very high officer he is,
he is not altogether savage. I think he is not a bad
man at all, and is even a God-fearing one, I
believe . . ."

Still inwardly composing his letter, Kristianpoller
cut his nails with his pocket-knife in honour of the
approaching Sabbath, and kept his eyes upon the
street to see whether or no more customers were on
the way. Suddenly his blood ran cold. He listened. Six
pistol shots—ah, how well he could distinguish between those and the report of guns!—were fired in
succession in his yard. All peaceful sounds died instantly—the quacking and cackling of the feathered
folk, the cheerful voices of the peasants, the whinnying of their little horses, the laughter of their women.
Through the window Kristianpoller saw their mouths
gape open and their hands go up to cross themselves.
In a moment they had all got down from the carts
where they had already taken their places, ready to
drive away. As though the sudden shots had hit the

day as well, the light seemed to go now very fast. The
glazier Nuchim's little room facing the bar across the
street was already in pitch darkness, although the windows stood wide open. Only the white table-cloth
shone out silverly, spread for the Sabbath.

A presentiment of evil prompted Kristianpoller to
leave his inn for the present, and by way of the window. He climbed out on to the street and slipped
across the way to the tumbledown blue cottage of the
glazier.

"They're shooting in my yard!" he said hastily.
"Don't light your candles. Bolt your door!"

And so they were, shooting in Kristianpoller's out-
house. Colonel Tarabas's own men, harmlessly confident of their own superiority, and in momentary expectation of their Sergeant-Major Kontsev, had begun
to go on drinking in company with the deserters from
the barracks, whereupon sleep and fatigue and even indifference soon overcame them. Gradually the false
camaraderie with which the old guard had baited the
deserters gave place to a temporary and ungenuine, but
nevertheless emotional friendliness. On both sides a
great many false but burning tears were shed. In a
word, they were all very drunk.

"Let's try a bit of shooting just to see if we can still
hit anything," said the cleverest of the deserting band,
one Ramzin.

"Splendid!" said the others.

"First let's draw some decent targets," said Ramzin. And he pulled a piece of chalk out of his trousers pocket, and set to work to draw all manner of large and smaller figures on the dark-blue distempered wall. This Ramzin was a skilful fellow. He had always been good at every kind of trick, including conjuring and sleight-of-hand. His tall, gaunt figure, the black eyes in his sallow face, his long and crooked nose with a list to one side, the raven-black mane of hair which, not without vanity, he allowed to fall in disorder over his forehead, and his long, bony hands with the slightly bent fingers, had long since given rise to the suspicion in his comrades' minds that he could not be really one of them. Some had known him two years and more, and had seen service with him. He had never told any of them which government or province he belonged to. And all at once, most of them having taken him for a Ukrainian, he seemed to belong just here, in this brand-new country. Its language seemed to be his mother-tongue. He spoke it fluently and with raciness.

He was an adept with his chalk, they all agreed—his drawings were masterly in their eyes. They had ceased to feel tired. They crowded in a dense clump behind Ramzin, standing on tip-toe to follow the agile movements of his hand. Against the deep blue background of the wall Ramzin evoked snow-white kittens chasing mice, raging, greedy dogs which likewise filled the

mice with terror, men having at the dogs with sticks.
Below these in another row Ramzin began to draw
three women, unmistakably in the act of taking off
their clothes. To the onlookers Ramzin's hand, somewhat lustful and certainly impatient as it was, seemed
with extreme dexterity to divest the bodies of their
garments in the very moment of clothing them; he
stripped the women in the same second as he created
them, and this proceeding excited and embarrassed the
audience in equal measure. They were all at once completely sober. But another and far more potent intoxication now possessed them. Each one wished that Ramzin would stop, or change the subject of his pictures,
but at the same time and just as ardently they wished
him to continue. They were in a turmoil of fear and
shame, intoxication and expectancy. Their eyes, before which all the pictures now and then hung blurred,
looked again in the next instant and saw in sharp
and torturing distinctness the shadows and lines of the
bodies, the nipples on the breasts, the tender firmness
of the thighs, and the delicate fragility of the slim and
charming ankles. With scarlet faces, and in order to
overcome the uneasiness whose helpless slaves they
were, the men began to utter witless, meaningless, and
shameless cries. Some whistled piercingly, others burst
out into loud neighing laughter. Now upon the wall
on which Ramzin was completing his infernal task,
fell the farewell glory of the sunset. The wall was bur-

nished gold and azure, and in the golden blue the
chalk-white figures seemed to be carved, not sketched.
Ramzin stepped back. He suddenly stopped short in
the midst of filling his third row with German soldiers
of different corps, soldiers of the Red Army, and every
kind of symbol such as sickle and hammer, eagle,
double-headed eagle, and the like. He hurled the chalk
against the wall. It smashed and fell in many fragments to the floor. Ramzin turned round. Next to him
stood the Ukrainian Kolohin, one of Tarabas's own
men. Ramzin pulled the pistol out of the other's belt.

"Out of the way!" he said.

They made way for him. Ramzin retreated to the
open doorway, took aim, and shot. He hit all the six
pictures in succession, the whole of the top row. There
was applause. They stamped their booted feet upon the
ground. They shouted: "Bravo!" and "Well done,
Ramzin!"

Now each was impatient to get a gun into his hand.
Tarabas's men shot first, then handed their pistols to
the strangers. They all tried, and every one of them
missed.

"They're bewitched," said someone. "Ramzin's bewitched his pictures!"

The very devil was in it. Even the good shots whose
hand and eye had never failed them fired too high or
too low now. After a few more bullets had gone wide,
they told themselves that an invisible presence touched

the weapons in the instant when the ball left the barrel. Now Ramzin shot again. He did not miss. He had certainly drunk no less than all the rest. They had seen what he had had. How came it, then, that his hand was more sure than every other hand? Ramzin chose his target, took aim, shot, and hit it. Yes, as though goaded by some diabolical command, he began to ask the others to tell him the exact spot they wanted him to hit. The questions aroused in most of them the lust of sheer destruction, a hot and smouldering desire to see certain parts of the naked, ever more naked, bodies of the three women struck by the bullets and exterminated. Ramzin's first question as to what his target should be remained unanswered. Shame and passion choked them. Ramzin helped them on.

"Left breast of the third one from the middle, second woman?" he asked; or: "The hem of her chemise?" "Ankle or nipple?" "Face?" "Nose?"

Gradually it became impossible to withstand the questions which found out their most secret wishes even more accurately than the marksman's eye infallibly found its target in the pictures. Ramzin's shameless questions called forth answers as shameless. Ramzin shot, and missed not one of all the targets that they called to him to put a bullet through.

Little by little the yard was filled with curious peasants, attracted by the gay crack of the shots and the men's guffaws. What they saw confused them utterly.

Now they had all deserted their little carts. They stood there with their mouths and eyes and ears wide open. They pushed and stretched the better to see what was taking place there in the out-house.

Suddenly Ramzin, having disposed of three full rounds of ammunition, called out: "Give me a rifle!"

They brought him one. He aimed and pulled the trigger. Scarcely had the sound of the shot died away when a cry went up from every throat. A large patch of blue-distempered lime, bearing the last four of Ramzin's obscene drawings, had loosed itself from the wall; it had sprung off and burst, and fallen to the ground in dust and fragments. And before the eyes of the dumfounded audience a veritable miracle took place —on the cracked surface of the wall, illumined by the deep golden brightness of the setting sun, there appeared, in place of Ramzin's carnal drawings, the mild, celestial countenance of the Virgin. They saw the face first, then the figure. Her heavy crown of hair was raven-black, a semi-circular silver diadem adorned it. Her black and beaming eyes seemed to look down upon the men with pain and sorrow beyond words, and yet with sisterly and blissful solace and child-like wonderment. The ivory skin gleamed against the carmine of her robe; one guessed the curve of the lovely, gracious bosom at which the little Saviour drew his sustenance. Burnished in the reflection of the setting sun, which on this day seemed loath to leave the sky,

the revelation of the Virgin's image in that place stood
before all of their eyes, a miracle of heaven; none could
doubt it.

Suddenly someone in the crowd began to sing in a
loud voice, fervent and deep and clear: "Mary, thou
sweet Mother," a hymn well known and loved in that
religious land, centuries old and born out of the people's hearts. Instantly, struck down by the lightning of
their faith, they fell upon their knees, the little peasants, the huge soldiers, the deserters and Tarabas's old
guard alike. An immense intoxication seized them.
They felt that they were floating in the air, whilst in
reality they knelt upon the ground. They felt a heav-
enly power grasp them by the shoulders and press
them down, but simultaneously it bore them to the
heights. The lower they bowed their backs the lighter
rose their souls to those high places. With vague, bewildered voices they joined in the hymn. All the songs
of praise to the Virgin sang themselves with their helpless tongues, and slowly, as they sang, the sunset faded
from the wall. Soon there remained of it only one
narrow beam, gilding her brow. It grew smaller and
smaller still. Now in the shadow of the room nothing
more shone except the mild countenance and the ivory
of the breast. The carmine robe mingled with the surrounding dusk. It was submerged in the oncoming
night.

They pressed forward towards the wondrous apparition. Many rose now from the ground where they had kneeled or lain prostrate. Others did not yet dare to stand. They slid and shuffled forward on their knees and bellies. In each one was the shuddering fear lest the miraculous image vanish no less suddenly than it had come. They tried to get as near to it as possible; they hoped that they might touch it with their hands. How long it was since their poor hearts had been vouchsafed a miracle like this! For years and years war had filled all the world! They sang every hymn to the Virgin they had learnt in school and church, as, standing, lying, kneeling, they approached the figure on the wall.

And suddenly the last gleam of daylight was gone, as though erased by an unseen, ruthless hand. The tender ivory of breast and throat and face, the silver crown, were now but pale shadows on the dark wall. Those who stood nearest rose and put out their hands to touch the Virgin's image.

"Stop!" cried a voice at the back of the room. It was Ramzin. Drawn up to his full height with the kneeling horde all round him, he stood there and cried out in a ringing voice: "Stop! Let no one touch it! This room is a church. That wall where you see that picture is where the altar used to be! The Jew removed it! He defiled the church. He painted the holy pictures over with blue lime. Pray, brothers, pray! Repent! This place shall be a church again. And the Jew Kristian-

poller shall do penance here as well. Let us find him
and bring him here. He is in hiding. But we shall find
him sure enough."

No one answered. It was now night. Through the
open door blue darkness poured into the room, strong
and cool. It intensified the terrible silence. The blue
wall had almost turned to black. Only a grey, irregular, jagged patch could still be seen upon it, nothing
else. The people who had not yet risen scrambled to
their feet at last, cautiously, as though they first must
loose the shackles from their limbs.

A wild fury, scarcely known even to themselves, im-
planted in their hearts from earliest childhood, caught
in the blood and driven into every vein, awoke now
and grew strong within them, fed by the alcohol they
had consumed that day, increased by the excitement of
the miracle they had experienced.

A hundred confused voices cried out for vengeance
for the mild, the gentle, the outraged and desecrated
Mother of God. Who had insulted her, smeared her
with cheap, blue lime and buried her in cement and
vodka-fumes? The Jew!—The ancient spectre, sown
thousandfold in the length and breadth of all the land,
the festering enemy in the flesh, incomprehensible,
nimble-witted, gentle and yet blood-thirsty, cruel and
yielding, more frightful than all the frightfulnesses of
the war that they had just been through—the Jew! In

that hour he bore the name of the inn-keeper Kristianpoller.

"Where is he hiding?" someone asked.

And others shouted: "Yes, where is he hiding?"

The peasants who had seen the Virgin's image
thought no more of returning home that night. But
others, too, who had only heard about the miracle,
now began to unharness their little horses and lead
them into Kristianpoller's yard. They seemed to think
it necessary to remain in a place where so divine an
event had taken place. Slowly at first, with their cautiously groping, quietly grinding minds they received
the wonderful tidings; they turned it about and about
in their stolid, churning brains, doubted its truth, grew
suddenly ecstatic, crossed themselves, gave praise to
God, and overflowed with hatred against the Jews.

Where could he be, the Jew Kristianpoller? A few
went into the bar to look for him. Behind the counter
they found only the servant, Fedya, quite drunk and
long since fast asleep. They looked for him in the
guest-rooms where the officers were quartered. Bed-
ding was tumbled, chests and cupboards opened.

Outside the inn and inside, in the yard, the people
gathered. Yes, even the peasants who had already
started on the road home turned back, eager to experience the miracle while there was still time. As they
drew up at the hotel in their little carts together with

their wives and children, they felt that they had not
come back into the town to worship before the benef-
icent apparition, but to be revenged upon the Jew who
had defiled the Mother of God. For the zeal of hatred
ever exceeds the zeal of faith, and is sprier and more
active than the devil. It seemed to the peasants that
they had not only seen the miraculous image, all of
them, with their own eyes, but also that they remembered in every smallest detail each sacrilegious action
by which the Jew had soiled the picture and covered
it with blue lime. And with their desire for revenge
there mingled now an obscure feeling of guilt which
they had laid upon their souls through being so heed-
less as to have let the Jew go his vile way in peace so
long. That much was clear—it was the devil who had
misled them into doing so.

They climbed down from their carts, armed with
whips and clubs, with the sickles, scythes, and knives
they had just bought. It was the hour when the Jews,
dressed in their best clothes, began to leave the synagogue, old men and cripples nearly all of them. Down
upon these the peasants now descended. The armed,
robust, infuriated men saw in the Jewish weaklings, in
these infirm and aged men, trailing home in all their
Sabbath helplessness, something particularly dangerous, more dangerous than health and wholeness, youth
and arms. Yes, in the Jews' unrhythmic trot, in the
stoop of their backs and the dark solemnity of their

long and gaping caftans, in their bowed heads, and even in the elusive shadows cast by their stumbling figures now here, now there, upon the road between the wooden sidewalks whenever they passed by one of the meagre oil-lanterns, in all these things the peasants thought they saw the truly hellish origin of this people that lived by trade and incendiarism, robbery and rapine.

As for the hobbling swarm of the poor Jews, they saw, or rather felt, catastrophe approaching. Only they stumbled on to meet it, half from sheer trust in the God they had just come from praising in the synagogue, and whom they felt at home and safe with (far too safe and far too much at home), and half paralysed by that cold fear with which nature in her cruelty has oppressed the weak, in order that they fall more surely prey to the power of the strong.

In the forefront of the peasants, whip in hand, strode one Pasternak, dignified to look upon with his tremendous bush of grey moustache. He belonged to the neighbourhood and was rich, and therefore doubly respected. When he came upon a level with the Jewish swarm, he raised his whip, swept the black and many-knotted thongs in a circle that cracked and whistled three or four times round his head, and then, his hand having caught the swing of it, he brought it down into the midst of the sombre bevy of the Jews. It struck a face or two. Here and there a cry went up. The entire

baffled swarm stopped still. Some tried to keep well up
against the walls of the houses and vanish in their
shadow. Others, however, flung themselves down from
the yard-high wooden sidewalk into the road before the
peasants' very feet. They picked them up and threw
them into the air. Dozens of hands stretched out to
catch the spinning Jews and toss them up again, and
yet again, and for a fourth time.

The night was very clear. Against the star-strewn
azure of the sky, the dense black, flapping figures of
the Jews, fluttering up and falling down again, were
like strange night-birds of enormous size. Like night-
birds', too, were the short, shrill cries they uttered.
Their tormentors answered them with bellowing
laughter. Here and there a waiting woman opened a
shutter at a Jewish window, to close it instantly again.

"All Jews to Kristianpoller's yard to kneel down and
pray!" cried out a voice. It was Ramzin's. And Pasternak drove them with his whip down from the sidewalk. The peasants marched them in their midst to
Kristianpoller's.

In the out-house where the miracle had occurred two
candles had now been lighted. They were stuck upon
a log of wood and lit the Virgin's face with their un-
certain flame. All the soldiers, the followers of Colonel
Tarabas as well, knelt down before the candles, sang,
prayed, crossed themselves, bowed their heads, and
struck their foreheads against the ground. The candles,

continually renewed—no one could tell where they all
had come from; it was as though every peasant had
brought candles with him to Koropta—shed shadow
rather than light. A solemn darkness reigned within
the room, a darkness of which the two candles were
the shining core. It smelt of cheap tallow, of sweat and
leather, of acrid sheepskin and the hot breath of open
mouths. Above their heads in a deep dusk, in the impotent, wavering light of the weak flames, the gentle,
wondrous countenance of the Madonna seemed now
to weep and now to smile consolingly, above all to live,
in a sublime reality not of earth, to live.

When the peasants arrived with the black swarm of
Jews, Ramzin cried: "Room for the Jews!" And the
kneeling, prostrate crowd made a lane for them to pass
down. As the poor creatures, singly and in pairs, were
shoved and prodded forward, it happened that this and
that one of the peasant worshippers interrupted his devotions to spit at them. The nearer the Jews came towards the miracle, the more violently and often were
their dark garments spat upon, and soon their caftans
were stuck over and over with clots of silvery spittle,
yellowish slime, a frightful and abstruse kind of crazy
buttons. It was ludicrous and horrible.

They forced the Jews to kneel. And as they knelt,
turning their lost and anxious eyes to right and left, as
if to learn from which side still greater peril was about
to fall upon them, and, filled with panic terror of the

candles and the picture they illumined, tried to turn their heads away, Ramzin shouted suddenly from the back of the room: "Sing!"

And as the faithful, for close on the fiftieth time, intoned the Ave Maria once again, the Jews, in mortal fear, began to give forth ghastly sounds from their strangling throats, like the broken tune of a decrepit hurdy-gurdy, and bearing no resemblance to the anthem.

"Down on your faces!" Ramzin commanded. And the obedient Jews touched the floor with their fore-heads. They held their caps clutched fast in their hands, as though they were the last symbols of their own faith which they were to be robbed of.

"Get up!" cried Ramzin. The Jews got up, feebly and absurdly hoping that they were now delivered from their torture.

"Come on, all!" said Ramzin's fearful voice again. "We'll take them home!"

And most of the worshippers left the scene of grace. Soldiers in uniform and peasants with lashes, sticks, and sickles in their hands drove the dark flock of Jews through the dimly lighted street. They broke into each one of the little houses, putting out the lamps and candles and commanding the Jews to relight them, be-cause they knew that they were forbidden by their law to kindle fire on the Sabbath.

Many of the peasants took the burning candles out

of their stands, hid the stands under their coats, and amused themselves with holding the candles to every inflammable stuff in reach. Thus very soon curtains and table-cloths and sheets were all in flames.

The Jewish children set up a pitiable wailing; the Jewish women tore their hair and called upon their men-folk by their names, the sound of which seemed to the tormentors silly and contemptible, and made them laugh until the tears came. Not a few mimicked the crying of the children and the women. An insane tumult rose into the night. A few of the captive Jews made a childish attempt to hide themselves in the familiar houses. But they were quickly caught and beaten.

"Where is your inn-keeper Kristianpoller?" this and that voice would roar at intervals.

Immeasurable though the din had now become, that fearful question reached the ears of everyone, despite the general chaos. And as now the Jews, together with their wives and children, in a wild chorus, and calling on every holy thing to bear them witness, began, one and all, to swear that they did not know where their brother Kristianpoller was, the cruel questions fell thicker and faster.

"All right, we'll make you!" cried someone in the crowd. It was one of the soldiers, a gigantic fellow with broad shoulders and a tiny head that seemed to be no bigger than a nut, a puny fruit upon a mighty tree. He pushed the crowd aside, strode forward, and stood before a young Jewish woman, whose dark and comely face, with the innocent hazel eyes wide with terror beneath the shimmering white silken kerchief, may have attracted him from afar and aroused in him both love and hate. Fear paralysed her. She did not even try to move away.

"This is his wife! Here's the blackguard Kristianpoller's wife!" shouted the soldier.

An unspeakable, inhuman lust inflamed his tiny, pallid, hairless face. He raised a short wooden club and brought it down upon the Jewess's head. It felled her instantly. Everyone cried out. Blood showed upon the kerchief's shimmering white. And as though the sight of the red blood, the first of that day's shedding, had lent clear meaning and direction to their vague and smouldering fury, now in the others, too, awoke an invincible desire to strike, to trample underfoot. Red veils of blood already hung before their eyes, streaming red veils like bloody waterfalls. They struck at random, each with whatever he chanced to have in his hand, and their blows fell on the men, the women, and the children, even on inanimate objects within range.

Kontsev, arriving from the barracks with a small platoon, could see at once that he could not cope with the trouble in the town. He sent word post-haste back to Colonel Tarabas, meanwhile addressing the crowd in various languages, shouting alternate threats and reassurance to them above the great commotion. The peasants and the soldiers were, however, too far gone in their delirium to understand or to be sobered by his words. They merely felt obscurely that some force of order was moving their way, inimical therefore, and set themselves to oppose it energetically. The implements with which they had just been laying about them they now employed as missiles against Kontsev and his troop. Kontsev feared to risk giving a decisive command without his colonel's leave. He decided, therefore, to retreat for the time being, distributing his men on either side of the street to guard such houses as had so far escaped attack. Nor did the crowd attempt to advance. With all the greater violence they turned back on the Jews around them, and on the captives in their midst. Here and there blue flames went up from the interior of the houses, and through doors and windows came screams and wailing. Kontsev waited impatiently. Colonel Tarabas must come any moment now.

But only Kontsev's messenger came back. He reported that all the officers both in the mess and in their sleeping-quarters were in a state of almost complete inanimation, and that not even the mighty Colonel Tarabas differed, at that moment, from the rest. On the contrary, his condition was, if anything, worse. For as the cook and the soldiers on duty in the mess had told him, there had been a fight in the late afternoon.

Old Major Kisilaika, the one whom they had found
in charge of the station when they first arrived, left
over from the old days and in no mind since to resign,
had called across the room to Colonel Tarabas that the
kind of reckless drinking which went on there was a
thing unknown in the old Russian army. Out of this
remark a fracas had arisen. Tarabas had invited all the
dissatisfied to leave the new army on the spot. Thereupon the officers had started fighting, Tarabas as well.
And then there had been a surprising reconciliation all
round, the result of which had been a fresh outbreak of
the desire to drink until they could hold no more.

Sergeant-Major Kontsev decided to gather his small
platoon together and tackle the mob of peasants with
fixed bayonets. He was not yet aware that there were
soldiers in the crowd. Some of these still had the pistols
with them which they had fired at Ramzin's drawings.
They hated Kontsev. They had not forgotten one iota
of what he had done to them. They recognized him by
his voice, and with Ramzin's encouragement decided
that their moment of revenge was come. They pushed
the peasants out of their way and placed themselves in
the forefront of the mob. As Kontsev gave the command to advance, Ramzin shot, and the deserters followed suit. Three of Kontsev's men went down. He
realized the danger, but it was too late. Before he could
cry "Fire!" to his troops, Ramzin and the deserters had
pushed forward and discharged the remainder of their

ammunition, to the triumphant yells of the drunken peasants.

Three or four oil-lanterns only lit the street, but now from time to time, ever more frequently, thin tongues of flame shot out from the Jews' houses, casting a feeble, intermittent shine into the darkness where a short and fierce hand-to-hand encounter now began. Old soldier that he was, Sergeant-Major Kontsev clearly foresaw the outcome of this fight. He knew that his small troop was no match for that infuriated mob. Shame and grief filled him at the thought of the inglorious end awaiting him in this inglorious brawl, him, than whom the mighty Russian army had had no more intrepid soldier. Many another soldier, honourable foes both Austrian and German, he had killed with his honourable soldier's hands. He had come to this place partly because he had not known where else to go, but partly, too, out of devotion to his master and colonel, Tarabas. What was this new little country to Kontsev? What in the devil's name were the Koropta Jews to him?—Ah, what an end for an old soldier who had fought in the great war! All these thoughts coursed with great rapidity through grand old Kontsev's mind while his well-trained soldier's conscience, like a separate brain—his real one—dictated all the measures to him which this most hideous situation called for. A pistol in his left hand, and in his right the great curved sabre, with the yelling peasants and the deserters, his mortal enemies, all round him, the courageous Kontsev shot and thrust on every side at once. He towered over the besetting horde by his whole powerful and massive head. In every region of his body he felt pain; blow upon blow hailed down upon him. Suddenly he felt something pierce his throat. Dense clouds now hung before his blood-shot eyes, but he could just distinguish Ramzin, with an ordinary peasant's jack-knife in his upraised hand.

"Dog," Kontsev said, the death-rattle in his throat. "Son and grandson of a bitch!"

With the last gleam of consciousness vouchsafed him by approaching death Kontsev grasped the ignominious manner of his going. A peasant's knife had gone into his throat. A despicable bandit had wielded it. Shame, bitterness, and hate distorted his features. He sank down, first upon his knees. Then his arms went out; they fell back to give him room. He had not strength enough to support himself upon his hands. He fell forward and lay at his full length, his face in the slime and litter of the road. The blood streamed out of his neck, it overflowed the collar of his tunic and soaked into the mud.

Over his corpse and over the corpse of the other soldiers the mob's hobnailed boots trampled and stamped. Some bore self-inflicted wounds, others had been injured. But the sight of their own blood did not in the least appease them; it mounted to their heads even more potently than the other blood which they saw flowing round them. Just as the brief battle had not tired them, but on the contrary had only increased their blind urge to destroy. Out of their cavernously gaping mouths came, in a strange and regular, almost a strict rhythm, inhuman cries, in which sobs and wailing, triumph, grief, weeping and laughter, and the cries of wild beasts in heat and hunger, all were mingled.

One of the soldiers suddenly produced a torch. He had wound a table-cloth round his stick, smashed one of the street-lanterns, drenched the cloth with oil and set it alight. First he made passes with the torch over the heads of the crowd, then he put it first to one of the low, overhanging cottage roofs, then to another. They were shingle-roofs and very dry. Many now followed his example, and gradually the whole Koropta high street had begun to burn.

The licking flames dancing so gaily on the roofs to right and left all the way up and down the street delighted the mob so much that they almost forgot the Jews. True, they still dragged the poor captives with them. When these stumbled and fell to their knees, which they did continually, they were wrenched roughly up again, but they were no longer kicked about or beaten. Their captors even began to talk to them with heartening and pacifying words, and to draw their attention to the gruesome beauties of the night's performance.

"Look, look at those little flames!" they said. "See this wound!" they said. "It hurts, I can tell you!" they said.

They had got used to the Jews, gradually. These had become, after the long-drawn torture they had been put through, an indispensable element in the triumphal procession. They could on no account be spared.

But the harmless words and gentle treatment frightened the Jews still more than blows and torments. They thought that the general mildness could be but a prelude to still more atrocious agonies to come. A peaceful hand moving towards their shoulders sent them cringing back as before a whip. They looked like a clump of madmen; they seemed to represent a special kind of stolid, feeble, anxious lunacy, amidst the dangerous and violent insanity of the others. They saw their houses burning; perhaps their wives and children, and their children's children might be dead now; they would have gladly prayed, but they were afraid to utter the least sound. Why did their ancient God punish them so? For four long years He had heaped horror upon horror on the Jews of Koropta. The Tsar, the old Pharaoh, was dead; a new one had arisen in the eternal land of Egypt, yes, a perfectly new and very small, but most unnaturally cruel Egypt had replaced the old. Stifled sighs escaped their lips from time to time; they sounded like the hoarse and frightened crying of sea-gulls before a storm.

The guard on duty at the barracks had heard the shooting. So had the rest of Tarabas's men, who had remained behind in Kristianpoller's out-house. These awoke precipitately out of the drunken state into which alcohol, the miracle, the praying and the singing had put them. Fear seized upon them, fear of the trained soldier brought to book by his own soldier's conscience, and dread of punishment at Tarabas's terrible hands. Some of their weapons had gone with the deserters.

The soldiers in the out-house looked at each other silently, reproachfully, apprehensively; their eyes fell before each other's eyes in consciousness of guilt. Now that their minds were cleared of the beclouding fumes they could recall each episode of this strange and dreadful day, but the evil spell which had been laid upon them remained inexplicable.

Innumerable candles still burnt and smoked before the Virgin's image. But it had become invisible. It was as though it had gone away again, engulfed in the surrounding shadow.

"There's hell let loose out there," one of the soldiers began at last. "We'd best get back to barracks. We ought to let the old man know. Who'll risk it?" There was no answer.

"Let's all go together," said another.

They put out the guttering candles with their fingers, and left the out-house. They saw the reflection of the

fire, heard the commotion, broke into a run and set off
for the barracks, giving the high street a wide berth.
When they arrived, the regiment was drawn up in
readiness to march. Tarabas was just about to mount
his horse.

"Fall in, quick!" he shouted to them.

They ran inside, looked for and found a few forgotten carbines, and pushed their way into the column
wherever they could find a place.

A few of the officers, not all, were on their feet again.
The usual commands were given. The depleted regiment marched towards the town, Tarabas on horse-
back at its head, as prescribed, with drawn sword. They
made straight for the high street.

The mighty Colonel Tarabas, twenty paces in advance of his first platoon, red in the light of the flames,
was so terrible to see that the whole crazy mob was
stricken dumb.

"Back!" thundered Tarabas.

And obediently they all began to back, still facing
him. But suddenly they turned, as though the realiza-
tion had come to them in a flash that walking backwards they could never hope to escape the awful Tarabas in time, or the innumerable fixed bayonets behind
him, glinting in the firelight. They scattered headlong,
running for their lives.

They left the Jews behind; they had forgotten them.
The abandoned captives stood there huddled close

against each other, like a black, glued-together bundle
in the middle of the street. They sensed that rescue had
arrived, but knew as well that it had come too late.
They were lost, utterly and for all time. They did not
move. Now let the rescuers trample and stamp them
down to the end. Death and a mortal chill were in their
hearts. They had ceased to feel even their physical hurts.
Along the board sidewalks, where the fire had already
taken foothold here and there, stood women and children with their burning houses behind them. They
screamed no more. Even the children had done with
crying.

"Out of the street!" commanded Tarabas. And before him the compact swarm of Jews dispersed to right
and left; and the wooden planks echoed to the sound
of the women's and children's fleeing footsteps.

The street cleared, the soldiers now began to salvage
what they could out of the houses. They tried as best
they could to quench the fires. But there was lack of
water and containers. It was a hopeless undertaking.
They threw coats, stones, mud upon the flames; not
looking what it was they seized, they brought bed-
clothes and tables, candlesticks, lamps and pots, racks,
cradles, bread and every kind of foodstuffs, household
utensils of all species, out of the houses. The smouldering places on the sidewalks they trod out with their
boots. What they could not extinguish they left to burn;
they tried to wrench the burning roof-tiles loose with

bayonet, sword, and rifle-butt; they tried to batter
down the burning walls, and stamp the fire out of
flaming bed-clothes.

An hour later there was nothing to be seen but the
last blue flickering, yellow smouldering, red subsiding
embers of the wholly and partly gutted houses of
Koropta, and the blue-grey, suffocating smoke en-
veloping the town. Tired out, inert, the soldiers lay and
sat about in the street. Fortunately there was not a
breath of wind. Of the few houses which the fire had
spared, only one still sheltered living inhabitants—the
inn of the White Eagle, the inn of the vanished Jew
Kristianpoller. Hither, in the yard and in the rooms,
in the spacious parlour and in the cellar, Jews and
peasants had come, and were coming still in crowds.
Fright and fatigue, drink and the deafening uproar
and their pains, had put a number of them to sleep.
The peasants and the Jews lay side by side. There were
no more soldiers in sight. The deserters, under Ramzin's leadership, had already left Koropta. Some of the
children screamed out in their sleep, women were
weeping. A few Jews sat cowered together on the floor,
unable to summon strength enough to rise, humming
and murmuring their prayers, and rocking back and
forward to the rhythm of their ancient melodies.

When the dawn came, a fair dawn heralding another
of the golden days of that protracted and unusual autumn, the peasants were the first to wake. They rose

somewhat unsteadily to their feet, woke their wives, and went out to see after their carts and horses. Dully and laggingly remembrance of the evening came back to them, and of the night, the fire, the fight, the miracle, and the Jews. They went into the out-house. And lo! the marvellous picture of the Madonna was still there upon the wall; innumerable logs lay on the ground beneath it, and on the logs were stuck innumerable burnt-out stumps of candles.

So it was true, then. The Virgin's mild countenance was unaltered in the grey light of the morning. Tender, smiling, grieved, it rose in luminous ivory above the crimson robe. Its tenderness, its pain, its divine sadness, its celestial beauty, were more real than the morning, than the rising sun, than the memory of the bloody, fiery terrors of the night. The memory of all those things vanished before the picture's holiness. And if in this or that one of the peasants there was a stirring of remorse, he felt that everything was pardoned in that it was vouchsafed him to look upon the lovely countenance.

For all that—they were peasants. They thought of their farmyards and their farms, of the pigs and of the money in the bags around their necks. They must get home, back to their various villages in the neighbourhood. And they made double, triple haste to do so, for those who had remained behind at home must now receive the tidings of the miracle in Koropta. And

simultaneously the thought lay in their minds that
there might still be danger in store from Colonel Tarabas and the regiment which they had somehow managed to escape by flight the night before. They climbed
into their little carts. They whipped up their little
horses and galloped away towards the neighbouring
villages.

When Colonel Tarabas entered the Kristianpoller
inn, he found there only the unhappy Jews; they came
to meet him with lacerated, desperate faces drawn
with weeping, hands uplifted in entreaty, nameless
pain and terror in their eyes. He ordered them to leave
the inn, to betake themselves to such houses as were
still whole and not to show themselves or move from
there before they received new orders to do so. And
because they stirred his pity, he gave them his assurance that the soldiers would keep guard over their
safety so long as they stayed shut up inside the houses,
and quite still. They departed.

One or two officers arrived. Tarabas went with them
into the out-house to see the miraculous picture of the
Madonna. They bared their heads before it. Tarabas's
soldiers had told how Ramzin had shot at his indecent
drawings, and how this picture had suddenly appeared
from behind the plaster of the wall. Tarabas crossed
himself. His first impulse was to kneel. But he reflected
swiftly that it was incumbent upon him to maintain
an attitude of sober common sense after the incidents

of the previous night, which were the murderous consequence of all too blind belief. Behind him stood his officers. He was ashamed. He must not by the slightest gesture betray the bigotry within him. He crossed himself again and turned, and left.

In Tarabas's opinion the inn-keeper Kristianpoller was of a certainty in hiding somewhere in the building. He ordered every nook and cranny to be searched. Meanwhile they were bringing in the soldiers who had been killed that night. There were five of them, Kontsev among the rest.

"Take Kontsev to my room!" commanded Colonel Tarabas.

He gave a few instructions for the next hour. He ordered them to connect him by telephone with the capital, he wished to speak to General Lakubeit. Then he went into his own room, bolted the door, and sat down by the bed on which the dead Kontsev had been laid.

PART TWO

FULFILMENT

16

NOW Tarabas was alone with the dead Kontsev.
They had washed the face, cleaned the uniform of the
traces of blood and mud, polished the high boots,
brushed the mighty moustache. Sword and pistol lay
beside him, to the right and to the left; the powerful,
hairy hands with their large and damaged finger-nails
were folded low over the body. The eternal peace into
which he had entered hovered over the soldierly, sharp
features with a softening shine. But the features of
Colonel Tarabas wore an expression of bitterness and
unrest and distraction. He wished that he could weep,
that he might give way to an insane fit of rage. But
Colonel Tarabas could not weep. He noticed that the
sergeant-major was grey at the temples; he passed his
hand over the grey hair at the temples, but drew it
away at once, taken aback by his own tenderness. He
thought about the gipsy's prophecy. Nothing so far
announced his saintliness!

Foolish words, buried long since under the weight of
fearful happenings, drowned in the blood that one had
shed, submerged, like the years in New York, the
café-owner, the girl Katharina, Cousin Maria, father,

mother, and home! Tarabas tried hard to call these
pictures that rose before him "memories," and thus to
deprive them of their power. These thoughts that had
come now to torture him, he would gladly have given
them those trivial titles which would have stamped
them as mere harmless, insignificant shadows of the
past, no sooner come than gone again. He tried to take
flight before them in his bitterness at the death of
Kontsev, the best man he had, and to lash up his
thirst to be revenged for that death. Now he hated
them all, these Jews, these peasants, this Koropta, this
regiment, this whole new country, this peace, this revolution which had brought it forth and made it what
it was. What should he do? Ah yes—how rapid were
all Tarabas's decisions!—he would put things in order
first and then resign, tell little General Lakubeit a
home truth or two, and then get up and go! Get up
and go! But where to, mighty Tarabas? Was there
still an America? Was there still the house where he
was born? Where was home? Was there no war anywhere in all the world?

Tarabas was roused out of these meditations—they
were, as one can see, nothing but ideas in an incoherent
chain—by the orderly's voice announcing through the
closed door that the call for General Lakubeit would
come through in twenty minutes, and would the
colonel kindly go down to the post-office to receive it.
Tarabas swore at the primitive and inconvenient postal

arrangements—another evil consequence of founding
new and superfluous states. He ordered candles, a vigil
for the dead, a priest, and departed for the post-office.
He sent away the single clerk on duty, saying that he
had business of state to conduct. The clerk went away.

The telephone rang and the colonel himself took up
the receiver.

"General Lakubeit!"

Tarabas prepared to give a brief report.

But the distinct, soft voice of the little general, sound-
ing as though it came from the life beyond, said: "Don't
interrupt!" And thereupon proceeded to give short and
concise instructions: the regiment was to be held in
readiness, reinforcements from the distant garrison at
Ladka could not be sent out for another forty-eight
hours; fresh outbreaks were to be expected; all the
peasants of the district were gathering, to go and see
the miracle; the local priest must be asked to keep the
people quiet; all Jews were to remain inside their
houses—"so far as there are any left," those were the
general's actual words—and Colonel Tarabas caught the
rebuke and scorn of the remark.

"That is all!" the general concluded; then "Wait a
minute!" he called.

Tarabas waited.

"Repeat, please!" commanded Lakubeit.

Tarabas went rigid with rage and fright. He repeated
obediently.

"That'll do!" said Lakubeit.

Thunderstruck, impotent and full of rage, annihilated by the feeble, distant voice of a feeble old man, not even a soldier but "only a lawyer" at that, the mighty Tarabas left the post-office. It almost surprised him to be greeted by the clerk, who had been waiting outside the entrance. Strong in appearance but in reality weak and devoid of his old pride, the great Tarabas walked through the ruins of the little town of Koropta. On either side of the high street were places where the fire still smoked and smouldered. And Tarabas, in spite of the undoubted tangibility of his flesh and muscle, looked like a gigantic ghost moving amidst the ashes and the debris and the needlessly salvaged, ownerless objects in miscellaneous heaps outside the houses.

Without a glance towards the soldiers, he went back into the inn. Astonishment brought him to a standstill in the parlour, for behind the bar, nodding and bowing as though nothing had happened, stood the Jew Kristianpoller. As though nothing had happened, the servant Fedya was washing up the glasses.

At the sight of the Jew, going about his everyday business as casual and unscathed as though suddenly emerged from behind a cloud which had hidden and protected him until that moment, a suspicion awoke in Tarabas that there might in fact be sorcerers among these Jews, and that this one actually was responsible for the desecration of the Madonna's image. The whole

great wall, the insuperable wall of clearest ice and cut
and polished hatred, of strangeness and mistrust, which
stands, no less today than a thousand years ago, between Jews and Christians, as though God himself had
put it there, rose now before the eyes of Tarabas. Visible through the transparency of the ice stood Kristianpoller, no longer a harmless fellow of an inn-keeper
and tradesman, no longer merely a contemptible but
harmless member of an inferior caste, but an alien, incomprehensible, mysterious personage, equipped with
hellish weapons for his war against men and saints,
against heaven and God. Out of the unfathomable deep
of Tarabas's mind rose now, as yesterday out of the
devout prostrations of the soldiers and peasants, unconscious of what currents flowed beneath their fervour, a
blind and lusting hatred of the Jew, scatheless now, and
emerging by some power unscathed for ever from every
other peril likewise. This time his name was Nathan
Kristianpoller. Another time it would be something
else. A third time he would have yet another name.
Upstairs in Tarabas's room lay his dear, good Kontsev,
dead to all eternity, and he had died for this immune
and diabolic Kristianpoller. Tarabas would have given
a hundred thousand Jews and more for one boot from
his dead Kontsev's foot! Tarabas did not return Kristianpoller's deferential greeting. He sat down. He did
not even order tea or vodka. He knew the man would
bring him something of his own accord.

And Kristianpoller did. He brought a glass of hot
and steaming golden tea. He knew that Tarabas was
not in the mood for alcohol at that moment. Tea is
calming. Tea clears the tangled mind, and in clarity is
no danger for reasonable men. It went through Tarabas's brain: He's cooked this tea in hell. How did he
know what I was wanting? When I came in I had
decided to order tea.—And yet, suspicion notwithstanding, the colonel felt it as a compliment that Kristianpoller had divined his wish. He could not deny the Jew
a certain admiration. He was moreover curious to learn
by what means Kristianpoller had contrived to hide
himself, and reappear this morning fresh and uncon-
cerned.

He began a cross-examination: "Do you know what's
been going on here?"

"Yes, Your Excellency!"

"It's your fault that your fellow-Jews were beaten
and ill-treated. Some of my men were killed in the
fighting. My good old Kontsev is dead—on your account! I'm going to have you hanged, my friend!
You're an inciter to rebellion, a desecrator of churches;
you're doing what you can to sabotage the new state
which took us centuries to get back again. Well, what
have you to say?"

"Your Excellency," said Kristianpoller, and he unbent his back and stood straight up, and looked the terrible one full in the face with his one good eye, "I have

incited no one to rebellion, I have desecrated no church,
nor anything belonging to one; I love this country as
much and as little as everybody else. May I make a
general remark, Your Excellency?"

"You may," said Tarabas.

"Your Excellency," said Kristianpoller, and bent his
back again, "I am only a Jew!"

"That's just the point," said Tarabas.

"Your Excellency," replied Kristianpoller, "I should
like most respectfully to mention that I became a Jew
through no will of my own."

Tarabas said nothing. It was no longer the terrible
Colonel Tarabas who sat there saying nothing, but
beginning to turn things over in his mind. It was the
youth Tarabas, thought to have died long since, once a
revolutionary, a member of a secret group which assas-
sinated the governor of Kherson; the student Tarabas
who had spent a thousand nights listening to discus-
sions; the pliable, passionate Tarabas, rebellious son of
a stony father, endowed with gifts of mind to think
and to consider, but also the Tarabas who never grew
and ripened, whose senses ruled and confused his head,
who plunged headlong into whatever came his way—
manslaughter, love or jealousy, or superstition, or war,
cruelty, drunkenness, or despair.

The cause which the Jew Kristianpoller defended
with his implacable common sense had nothing what-
soever to do with the mighty Tarabas and the

chequered career which had been his! And yet it shed
a light into the darknesses which had had Tarabas in
their possession for many years. Kristianpoller's answer fell upon the colonel's brain like a flash of light
into a cellar, illuminating for a moment lost and secret
depths, and corners full of shadow. And although the
colonel had meant, when he began his catechism, to
learn and elucidate the mysterious faculties of this uncanny Jew, now he was forced inwardly to confess
that Kristianpoller's answer had come like a sudden
beam of light, sooner to illuminate the darkness in his
own heart than that in which the Jew went wrapped,
together with all his strange race. For a while Tarabas
said nothing. For a moment his loud, heroic life showed
itself to him in all its worthlessness, stupidity, and
emptiness; he wondered if he ought not rather envy
the despised Kristianpoller his unfailing reason, and
the well-ordered existence that he doubtless led. The
moment of insight did not last. For in the mighty Tarabas that pride had not yet abated which crushes reason
in the minds of all the great ones of this earth, en-
veloping as in a cloud of spurious gold the rare intima-
tions of the truth which sometimes come to them.
Pride spoke now out of Tarabas:

"You let those other Jews, your brothers, be destroyed. If you had come forward, nothing would have
been done to them! Even your own people you be-

trayed! You're not worthy of the name of human being. I shall exterminate you!"

"Your Excellency," answered Kristianpoller, "those others would have all been beaten just the same, and I should have been killed. I have a wife and seven children. When Your Excellency came I sent them away to Kyrbitki, because I knew that there was danger. A new regime is always dangerous for us Jews. You are a noble gentleman, Your Excellency, I'm certain of it. But . . ."

Tarabas looked up and Kristianpoller broke off. He was in mortal terror of that "But" which had slipped out. He bowed again, and stood there with his back bent so low that the eyes of Tarabas, seated at the table, were on a level with the silk skull-cap worn by all Jews in the house.

" 'But' what?" asked Tarabas. "Out with it!"

"But," repeated Kristianpoller, and stood up straight once more, "but even you yourself, Your Excellency, are in God's hand. He guides us as He wishes us to go, and we know nothing. We do not understand His cruelty, nor His goodness either . . ."

"No philosophizing, Jew," Tarabas shouted. "Say what's in your mind, I tell you!"

"Well," said Kristianpoller, "Your Excellency spent too much time in the barracks yesterday." And after a while he added: "It was God's will."

"You're hiding behind God again," said Tarabas. "God's not your screen! I'm going to hang you, just the same. But first I want to know where you hid. And you're to hide again. I have orders from headquarters to see that all Jews are kept out of sight. A lot of peasants are on their way here; they want to see the miracle in your yard. You'll be the first they'll slaughter, if they find you. But I'm going to have you hanged, and I want to see to that myself. Take care that my pleasure is not spoiled!"

"Your Excellency," said Kristianpoller. "The cellar is my hiding-place. My cellar is double-storied. I keep the spirits on the first floor. Underneath I have very old wine stored. At the bottom of the first staircase down there is a big flagstone, with a hook in it. I have an iron ring that fits into the hook, and an iron bar that goes into the ring. That's how I lift up the stone. When I'm in the lower cellar, I leave the tip of the iron bar between the trapdoor and the floor. Your Excellency can have me fetched out of that hiding-place and executed."

Tarabas said nothing. The Jew was not lying. But out of that mouth even the truth must contain some lie. Even the courage the inn-keeper Kristianpoller suddenly displayed must be a mask for some hidden cowardice, some devilish kind of cowardice. So Tarabas said: "You'll be fetched. And now I want to know why you defiled the church in your yard, and the Madonna's picture."

"It was not I!" cried Kristianpoller. "This house is very old. It came down to me from my great-grandfather. I don't know when they turned the chapel into a lumber-room. I don't know. I am innocent!"

These protestations of Nathan Kristianpoller's rang with such passion of sincerity that even Tarabas was moved to believe them.

"Very well! Now go and hide yourself," the colonel said. "And I want another room; I have had Kontsev put in mine."

"I have already seen to that," Kristianpoller answered. "I have given Your Excellency my late grandfather's room. It is on the second floor, next to the attic, I'm sorry to say. It is all ready. The bed is comfortable. The room is warmed. Fedya will show it to Your Excellency. I have put out a dozen candles for the late Sergeant-Major Kontsev. They are in the drawer of the pedestal beside the bed. The priest is upstairs, Your Excellency."

"Call him!" commanded Tarabas.

17

THE priest of Koropta was an old man. For more than thirty years he had had the cure of souls in this community. A simple, humble, and ungrateful labour. His ancient soutane, shiny with grease, hung slackly on his bony frame. The years had made him very small and thin; they had bent his back, and dug deep moats around his big, grey eyes, and furrows to either side of his narrow, toothless mouth; they had uncovered his brow and weakened his simple heart. He had seen the war come and go, the vast anger of heaven, and hundreds of mornings on which he could not read the mass. He had buried men who, struck down by chance bullets, had not been able to receive the final sacrament, and comforted the grief of parents whose children had been killed or died of injuries. And now his own desire was for death. Feeble and meagre, with extinguished eyes and trembling limbs, he appeared before Tarabas.

It was important, the colonel expounded, that the peasants who were approaching Koropta in force, athirst to see the miracle, be prevented from becoming excited. The harm already done was great enough.

The army counted on the influence of the clergy, and he, Colonel Tarabas, upon the help of Koropta's priest.

"Quite so!" said the priest. In the course of the past few years many new commanders had marched into Koropta, and spoken to him in words almost identical with those of Colonel Tarabas, and he had given all of them exactly the same answer—"Quite so!"

For a moment his big, light eyes turned their dim and ancient gaze upon the colonel's face. The priest felt pity for Colonel Tarabas. Yes, the priest was probably the only person in all Koropta who pitied Colonel Tarabas.

"I will speak to them tomorrow as you wish," he said.

But to Tarabas he seemed to have said this rather: "I know how it is with you, my son! You are bewildered and confused. You are powerful and powerless. You are brave but frightened. You give me instructions, but you know very well that you would feel much better if I could tell you what to do instead."

Tarabas said nothing. He waited for the old man to speak again. But he did not.

"Won't you drink something?" asked Tarabas.

"I should like a glass of water," said the priest.

Fedya brought it, and the old man drank a mouthful.

"Brandy!" called the colonel. Fedya brought this too; it was clear and colourless, like water. Tarabas tossed it off.

"Soldiers can stand a great deal of alcohol," said the priest.

"Yes, yes," answered Tarabas, absently. He felt strange and far away.

Both saw that there was nothing more to say. The priest was only waiting for a sign that he might go. There was much that Tarabas would gladly enough have said, for his heart was full; but it was also shut. A heavy sack, tied close about its secrets, so lay his heart in the breast of mighty Tarabas.

"What other orders have you for me, Colonel?" asked the priest.

"None, thank you," said Tarabas.

"Praise be to Jesus Christ," said the priest.

Tarabas too got up and whispered: "World without end, amen!"

18

ON that day, as so often before, there was drum-
ming and commanding in Koropta that the Jews must
not appear in the streets. Nor had they any desire to
do so. They sat in the few remaining houses of their
own people. They barricaded doors and windows. This
was, as far back as any of them could remember, their
saddest Saturday. But still they tried to console each
other and hope that God would soon send help to
them. They thanked Him for having at least left them
their lives. Some had been hurt. They sat about with
bound-up heads, with dislocated arms supported in
white slings, with lacerated faces on which the purple
lattice of the thongs was drawn, with naked chests and
backs and shoulders, about which damp towels had
been bound over the wounds. Even without these
further injuries they were weak or crippled, and all of
them old; the young and sound ones had been devoured
by the war. They did not feel the indignity that had
been put upon them, they were conscious only of their
pains. For the people of Israel has lived for twice a
thousand years under another indignity, compared
with which the later scorn and insults of its foes are

trivial merely—the indignity of knowing that there is in Jerusalem no temple. Whatever else of shame and ridicule and suffering may come their way is but the consequence of that bitter fact. Sometimes the Eternal One, as though the heavy cup of woe were not yet full, sends new punishments and plagues. Occasionally he employs the country-folk to serve His ends. There is no means of defence. But even if there were, ought one to take it? God willed that yesterday the Jews of Koropta should be beaten. And they were beaten. Had they not believed, in sinful exuberance, that peace was come again? Had they not ceased to be afraid? A Jew of Koropta has no right to be without fear.

They sat there, rocking their mauled bodies to and fro in the darkness of the little rooms, where the shutters had been nailed over the windows, although it is forbidden to knock nails in on the Sabbath. But the commandment to preserve life is as binding as that which enjoins the keeping holy of the Sabbath. They swayed and said the psalms aloud in sing-song, those that they knew by heart, and the others they read with their blurred eyes close against the pages of their books in the deep twilight of the rooms. Spectacles, broken and cracked, tied together with string, rested upon their long and sorrowful noses; they sat pressed close against each other to read, for the books were few, not more than one to every three or four of them. And they were careful not to raise their voices, for fear that they

might be heard outside. From time to time they stopped
and strained their ears for noises in the street. Some
even ventured to peep through the cracks and cross-
pieces of the shutters. Were they already there, the
new persecutors against whom the drums had warned
them? They must play dead; hope lay in making the
advancing horde of peasants think that not one Jew
had remained alive in Koropta.

Among these pitiable souls was the sexton of the
synagogue, Shemariah, of all unhappy Jews the most
unhappy. His woe was known to everyone. He had
been long years a widower, and had an only son. Yes—
had! For in reality he could no longer call his son by
that name, since—it happened during the war—he had
spat upon his father and announced his intention to
become a revolutionary. True, Shemariah, the father,
was to blame for it; he had saved up a few hundred
rubles with which to send his son to the university.
The foolish sexton of the Koropta synagogue had once
allowed himself the wish to see his son an educated
man, a doctor of medicine or law. But what had come
of this forward undertaking? An insubordinate school-
boy first, who had struck a master, been turned out of
the school, and then apprenticed to a watchmaker; who
founded a revolutionary "circle" in Koropta, repudiated God, read books, and prophesied the dictatorship
of the proletariat. Although he had a feeble constitution like his father, and the army would have none of

him, he enlisted as a volunteer—by no means in order
to defend his Tsar, but, as he declared, to "make a clean
sweep of all the despots." In addition to which he
stated that he did not believe in God because He was
only an invention of the Tsar's and the rabbis'.

"But you're a Jew, aren't you?" old Shemariah had
asked.

And "No, Father," the terrible son had answered, "I
am not!"

He had left home and gone to the war, and after
the outbreak of the first revolution wrote a last letter
to his old father, containing the information that he
would never come back home again. They were to
think of him as dead and done with.

Shemariah thought of him, accordingly, as dead and
done with, sat in mourning over him for seven days as
the law prescribed, and ceased to be a father.

He was poor in health and very thin, and, despite
his advanced age, still violently red of hair and beard.
He looked the picture of a wicked sorcerer with his
fan of bristling, flaming beard, the countless freckles on
his pale, bony face, the scraggy arms, long as a mon-
key's, and the long, limp hands, thin too and covered
with red hairs. He was called "Red Shemariah." And
many a Jewish woman went in fear of his yellow eyes.
But in reality he was a harmless man, resigned, humble,
simple, pious, good-humoured, and full of zeal and
diligence. He lived on onions, radishes, and bread. In

summer maize-cobs were his delicacy and luxury. His
income was the few copeks the congregation paid him,
and the occasional alms which came his way, mostly
on the eve of the holy days. For his son's end he
blamed himself. It was the punishment for his paternal
arrogance. True, he had now, according to the laws of
his religion, which was the only reality he recognized,
no son. But in his dreams and waking hours thoughts
of his child often came back to him. Perhaps he would
come back one day from the dead? Perhaps God would
send him home? To bring such things about one needs
but to be pious, ever more and more so. Therefore in
piety and observance of the law Shemariah surpassed
all others in the congregation.

Yesterday he, too, had been thrown up into the air
a few times. And someone's fist had struck against his
chin. Today his jaw gave him such pain that he could
hardly speak an intelligible word. But he gave his suf-
ferings no thought. Another care preoccupied him.
They had set fire to the little synagogue. Perhaps the
scrolls were burnt? And if they were not, should they
not be rescued now while there was still time? And if
they were, should they not now, as the law prescribes,
be buried in the cemetery?

All day long Shemariah's anxious thoughts hovered
round the scrolls. But jealousy kept him silent. He kept
his care a secret for fear lest there might be another
one besides himself prepared to save the sacred things.

But this magnificent deed should be reserved for him alone. In the great ledger in which the account of every Jew was kept in heaven, the Eternal One would enter a flourishing "Excellent" against his name, and fate might even bring him back his son as a reward. Therefore Shemariah kept his worry to himself. He did not know yet by what means it might be possible to reach the street without being seen by the soldiers of the dangerous Tarabas, or by the still more dangerous peasants. But the thought that the scrolls of the law, ruined by fire, should wait in vain for honourable burial, filled Shemariah with unspeakable anguish. If only he could talk about it! Pour out his heart! But the prospect of unique merit and a blest reward forbade him to utter a word.

Late in the afternoon, at the very hour when the Jews of Koropta were used on other days to celebrate the end of the Sabbath and the beginning of another week, loud noises penetrated to them through the fastened shutters. The peasants were coming, the peasants! Ah, these are no longer the more or less familiar and friendly neighbours from the villages around Koropta, although it was just those who had beaten one and thrown one into the air! But, ah! these are strange peasants, peasants never seen before. Everything conceivable and inconceivable can be expected from these —outrage of every kind, murder even. On second thought the cruelties of yesterday were jests, yes, posi-

tively harmless jests, when all was said and done! But
what might now come, that would certainly be dead
earnest.

The peasants were moving towards Koropta. They
were coming nearer and nearer, in long processions,
singing hymns. With many bright banners embroidered
in gold and silver, and led by white-robed priests, the
women and men, the girls and children came. There
were some among them who were not satisfied merely
to make the pilgrimage to Koropta. They had to make
the holy task still harder. Therefore they let themselves
fall down every five, seven, or ten paces, and shuffled
the next ten steps upon their knees. Others threw
themselves upon the ground at certain intervals, lay
there as long as it took to repeat a paternoster, rose,
staggered along a while, then fell again. Almost all
had candles in their hands. Their well-polished Sunday
boots were slung over their shoulders, to save the soles.
The women were wearing their brightest, prettiest kerchiefs; the men their Sunday vests embroidered with
gay flowers, which looked like the meadows of spring.
Shrill, out of tune and hoarse, but with voices warm
with fervour, they sent the miracle their songs still
from afar.

For the news of the wonder that had taken place in
Kristianpoller's yard spread through the villages of the
whole district within a single day. Yes, the manner and
the speed of this was a miracle in itself. Of the peasants

who had come to the Koropta market not a few had
driven to distant villages that same night to bring the
fabulous tidings to relatives, friends, and strangers
there. Certain events evoke an echo far and wide in
some inexplicable way, needing no aid from any of
the modern means of travel and communication to
make themselves known to all the world. The air trans-
mits the news to all whom it concerns. And word of the
miracle in Koropta went out thus and was heard for
miles around.

While the peasants thus approached from every side
at once, so that no less than six processions converged
at Kristianpoller's inn at the same moment; and while
the Jews in the few darkened houses sat longing for
the delivering night to come, Tarabas sat together with
his officers in the inn parlour, the servant Fedya waiting
on them in his master's stead. Kristianpoller had gone
into hiding.

But the pious peasants cherished no thoughts of
vengeance and violence today. They had taken the ad-
monitions of their priests to heart. Gently their ardour
flowed towards the miracle, like a full stream between
dikes. Services were held, several in close succession,
one for each group of pilgrims. An improvised altar
had been set up. The out-house recalled one of those
chapels, roughly and hastily erected hardly three hundred years before by the first missionaries to that land.

For three hundred years this people had been receiving
Christian baptism. And yet at the end of a day's gay
pig-market, and after a few rounds of beer, and at the
sight of a lame Jew, the ancient heathen woke in all
of them.

Things were not left wholly to the priests today; soldiers patrolled the street and all the lanes of Koropta.
Amongst the officers in Kristianpoller's parlour excitement reigned. For the first time since Tarabas had
taken over his command, they were daring to say in his
presence what they thought. Undeterred by his presence there, drinking his accustomed spirits, wrapped in
fierce gloom, and silent, they shouted and laughed
noisily, quarrelled and argued; some were expounding
various theories about the new state, the army, and
revolution, about religion, peasants, superstition, and
Jews. They seemed neither to fear nor to respect him,
all at once. It was as though the miracle in Kristianpoller's out-house and the Koropta fire had deprived
Colonel Tarabas of dignity and power.

The officers of the new regiment had come, like the
men, from all sections of the former army and the
front. They were Russians, Finns, Balts, Ukrainians,
Crimeans, Caucasians, and others. Accident and need
had swept them hither. They were soldiers, proper
mercenaries, taking service where they found it. All
that they wanted was to go on being soldiers, no matter

where. Without a uniform, without an army, they
could not live. And they needed, like all their kind no
matter where, a commanding officer without a weakness and without a fault, a visible weakness, that is, and
a visible fault. But yesterday Tarabas had quarrelled
with them; there had even been a fight. And they had
seen him drunk and senseless. They did not doubt that
in a few days he would be deposed. Moreover each
one of them believed that he himself was far more
capable than Tarabas or any other, to form a regiment
and to be its leader.

The silent Tarabas was well aware of what the officers were thinking. Suddenly it seemed to him that
until then his progress had been due only to luck, and
to no merit at all. He had exploited the accident of
his relationship to the War Minister, yes, more than
that, he had abused it. He had never really been a hero.
If he had shown courage, it was because his life was
worthless. He had been a good soldier in the war only
because he had wanted to die, and because in war death
is nearer than elsewhere. You have been leading a
wasted, ruined life, Tarabas, these many years. It began
in your third term as a student. You have never known
what was right for you. Home, Katharina, New York,
father and mother, Maria, the army and the war, all
lost! You were not even able to die, Tarabas! But you
let many others die; and many died by your own hand.

With pomp and in a masquerade of power you go about the world, but they have seen through you. The first to do so was General Lakubeit, then came the Jew Kristianpoller, and now the officers. And Kontsev, the only one that still believed in you, is dead.

So spoke Tarabas to himself. And soon it seemed to him that there were two Tarabases. Of these one stood by the table in a shabby, ash-grey coat; the mighty Tarabas sat at the table, armed, in uniform with all his medal-ribbons, booted and spurred. But the seated Tarabas was growing less and less, while the poor one on his feet in front of him and so humbly clad held his head high, and grew and grew.

Colonel Tarabas had ceased to listen to the conversation of the officers around him, so wholly did this poverty-stricken, proud image of himself preoccupy him. Suddenly he thought it seemed to be advising him to go upstairs to the dead Kontsev. He stumbled out of the room. He went upstairs, clinging to the banister. It was a long time before he reached the top. Then he went and stood beside the bed. He sent away the two soldiers who were keeping the dead-watch. Four great wax candles, two at the head and two at the feet, cast an unsteady, flickering, golden shine. There was a stuffy, sweetish smell in the room. A few drops of wax had fallen on Kontsev's shoulder. Tarabas scratched them off with his fingernail, and rubbed his sleeve over the dead man's tunic, brushing the last traces of the wax away. "Pray," came into his mind. Mechanically he recited one Our Father after another.

He opened the door, called the soldiers back, and went clumsily down the stairs again.

"Gentlemen," he said, "you are aware that the burial is to be tomorrow. At midday. Sergeant-Major Kontsev and the others."

It seemed to Colonel Tarabas that this announcement to his officers was one of the last that he would ever make, as though it were the hour of his own funeral that he had just informed them of.

He did not leave his table all that night. Something told him that he must wait there for the other Tarabas.

"He probably won't come again," said Tarabas to himself. "He won't have any more to do with me."

And he fell asleep, lying across the table with his head upon his folded arms.

19

A BLUE and silver Sunday morning, humming
golden bells and the choir of worshipping peasants still
in the out-house, woke Colonel Tarabas. He got up
immediately. Fedya was there already with the steaming tea, but Tarabas drank but a mouthful or two, impatiently. He was quite wide-awake and clear in his
mind. He could remember everything that had taken
place the day before. He recalled the conversation of
each of the officers. And every word the other Tarabas
had said to him stood distinctly in his memory. The
other Tarabas was real; the colonel doubted this no
longer. He went out into the high street. The soldiers
were resting beside the ruins of the houses. They rose
to their feet and saluted. A sergeant reported that the
night had been quiet. Tarabas said: "Good, good, very
good!" And went on.

The deep bells hummed, the peasants sang their
hymns.

Tarabas thought about the burial of Kontsev and the
others at midday. There was plenty of time; it was only
nine o'clock.

There was not a soul to be seen in Koropta, not a

single Jew. Not a sound from the few houses the fire
had left them, now bolted and shuttered with blind
windows.

"Perhaps they're all suffocated!" thought Tarabas.
Let them be suffocated, it was immaterial to him.

"It can't be immaterial to you," said the other Tarabas, however.

The colonel answered: "Yes, it is. I hate them."

Suddenly something black, suspicious, emerged from
one of the little houses. It vanished round a corner.

Tarabas might have fancied it; he went calmly on his
way.

But as he turned the next corner into a side street, a
perfectly terrifying apparition ran straight into his arms.

It was a radiant Sunday morning. The golden echo
of the bells still swung in the soft breeze. The peasants
were leaving the church upon the hill-top; the women's
bright kerchiefs shone out in many colours. It looked
as though the whole hill were moving down towards the
town, its slopes a mass of huge and brilliant flowers. A
gentle wind wafted the last notes of the organ into the
sky. The Sunday with the fading music of the organ
and the bells seemed one with sky and earth and all
that moved between them. Like the impious symbols
of an impious revolt against the laws of peaceful nature,
the razed places and the still smoking ruins in the town
showed black against the rest, a violation of this Sun-

day mood. The sunshine flooded the hill that rose to
the south-west of the little town. The moving flowers
seemed to crowd into an ever-denser carpet as the peasant women descended the slope. The yellow church
floated in a sea of sunlight. And upon its little tower
glittered the cross, gay and serene and holy, like an ex-
alted toy.

This was the aspect of the world, as the terrifying
apparition ran headlong into Tarabas.

This terrifying apparition was a skinny, wretched,
feeble, but nonetheless extraordinarily red-haired Jew.
Like a flaming garland the short beard surrounded his
pale, freckled face. On his head he wore a shimmering
skull-cap of black corded silk, now green with age, from
which fiery red curls escaped to join the flaming beard
on either cheek. The man's greenish-yellow eyes, sur-
mounted by thick red eyebrows like two tiny, blazing
brushes, seemed also to shoot forth flames, sparks of a
different kind, jets of icy fire. To Tarabas nothing
worse than this could happen on a Sunday.

His mind went back to that ill-fated other Sunday
from which his whole misfortune dated. That, too, had
been a glorious day like this one; in the Galician village, too, the church bells had been ringing when it
happened. And there, on the edge of the road, the new,
red-headed soldier had stood before him, the messenger
of doom. Ah! Had the mighty Colonel Tarabas imag-

ined that doom could be outwitted? That one could
escape it? That one could continue wars on one's own
account, when they were done and over?

A rufous Jew on Sunday morning! Hair of such red
as this, a beard like this, that did not merely flame but
positively blazed forth sparks, Tarabas had not seen in
all his life before, and there were few with eyes as
trained as his to distinguish red from red in hair. At
the sight of this Jew, Tarabas was not simply alarmed.
Alarm was what he had felt then, the first time, when
the new soldier greeted him. This time he was completely paralysed with horror. Of what avail were all
the battles he had fought? What did the terrors all
amount to now, those he had experienced and those
that he had caused? For now it was apparent that Tarabas bore the greatest terror of all these in himself, one
that he could not overcome, a fear that brought forth
other fears continually, a dread that fathered spectres,
and a weakness that created other weaknesses without
end. He had rushed from act of heroism into act of
heroism, mighty Tarabas! But not through his own
will; it was the fear in his heart that had driven him
through all those battles. Denying faith, he had lived
on superstition, brave out of fear, powerful out of
weakness.

Not less than the colonel's consternation was that of
the Jew Shemariah. He was carrying two scrolls in his
arms, like two dead children, each dressed in red velvet

embroidered with gold. The round wooden handles had been burnt, likewise the velvet hoods, leaving exposed the lower edges of the parchment which the fire had curled up and singed. Twice that day Shemariah had managed to convey scrolls to the cemetery, two each time. Before daybreak he had slipped out of the house. None of the soldiers had noticed him. He was convinced by now that God had specially appointed him, and him alone, to perform this holy work. Leaving the synagogue for the third time he had let imagination go so far as to believe, pitiful, credulous, simple as he was, that on this errand he was being kept invisible by that cloud of which the Bible tells. Meeting the colonel now, never doubting the cloud was round him, he stepped aside, as though thus to escape the mighty one unseen. This movement sent Tarabas into a frightful rage. He seized the Jew by the bosom of his caftan, gave him a shake, and thundered:

"What are you doing here?"

Shemariah did not answer.

"Don't you know you're all to stay indoors?"

Shemariah only nodded. At the same time he hugged the scrolls still closer to him, as though the colonel might try to take them from him.

"What's that you've got? What are you doing with those things?"

Shemariah, too terrified to utter a word, and moreover not very familiar with the language of the country, an-

swered by signs. When he had transferred the scroll
from his right arm on to his left one, he looked more like
a supernatural being than ever. Pressing his heavy burden to his breast with his weak left arm, he pointed with
his skinny right hand, overgrown likewise with red
stubble, to the ground, making the gesture of digging
and shovelling, then began to stamp and scrape with his
foot as though to smooth the fresh mound of a grave.
Most of this, naturally, Tarabas could not understand.
The obstinate silence of the Jew aroused his rage; it was
already rising dangerously.

"Talk!" he shouted, and lifted his clenched fist.

"Your honour!" stammered Shemariah. "See, they've
been burnt. They can't stay this way. They must be
buried. In the cemetery!" And he stuck out a hand in
the direction of the burial-ground of the Koropta Jews.

"Burying's none of your business!" thundered Tarabas.

Poor Shemariah, not quite understanding, thought he
was being called upon to give further explanations.
And he told, as best he could, stuttering and stammer-
ing, but radiant, how he had twice that day performed
his sacred duty. This, however, could but increase the
other's anger. For to Tarabas the fact that the Jew was
in the street now for the third time was a particularly
dreadful crime. It was the last straw. A Jew and red-
haired—on a week-day it might be overlooked; but a
Sunday made this apparition horrible and ghastly; and

a Sunday like this one made of it a horrible and ghastly personal affront to the colonel himself. Ah, poor, mighty, angry Tarabas!

All at once he felt the faint voice of the poor, other Tarabas. "Keep quiet! Keep quiet!" it said. But Tarabas, the mighty, did not listen. On the contrary, his rage increased.

"Be off!" he roared at the Jew. And as Shemariah went on standing there distraught and paralysed, Tarabas thrust out his hand and pushed the scrolls out of his arm. They fell with a thump to the ground, into the mire.

The next moment the appalling thing had happened. The crazed Shemariah put down his head and butted at the colonel's mighty breast, beating upon it with both his fists. He looked like a clown in a circus giving an imitation of a raving bull. It was absurd and heartbreaking to see. It was the first time since there had been Jews in Koropta that one of them had lifted up his hand against a colonel—and what a colonel! It was the first, and it was, in all likelihood, the last time, too.

Never in his life would Tarabas have believed that such a thing as this could happen to him. Had he needed any further proof that red-haired Jews on Sunday were his especial harbingers of evil, this attack would have furnished it in plenty. It was something different from an affront. It was—for something so impossible, it was impossible to find a word. If until this

moment Tarabas had been filled with bear-like rage,
there now began to seethe within him a fiendish, slow,
and cruel fury, an ingenious fury, resourceful, full of
cunning. A change came over Tarabas's face. All at
once it had turned very white. He smiled. Like a clamp
the smile lay between his lips, a cold, hard-frozen
clamp. With two fingers of his left hand he flicked the
red one off him. Then, with thumb and finger of his
right hand he gripped poor Shemariah by the ear-lobe
and pinched until a drop of blood appeared. This done
—still smiling—with both hands Tarabas seized the
fan-like, flaming beard. And with his whole gigantic
strength he began to shake the puny, quaking body to
and fro. A few of the hairs came out. He put them
calmly and without haste right and left into his coat-
pockets. He was still smiling, Colonel Tarabas! And
like a child who has found amusement in the destruction of a toy, and with a childish, almost idiotic expression in his eyes, he took the beard between his
hands again. Between the shakings, he spoke.

"You've got a son, haven't you? His hair's red, like
yours, eh?"

"Yes, yes," stammered Shemariah.

"He's a damned revolutionist!"

"Yes, yes," repeated Shemariah, while he was being
shaken to and fro, backwards and forwards, and each
separate hair upon his face felt like an open, yawning
wound. He wanted to repudiate his son; he wanted to

tell how his son himself had repudiated his father. But how to speak? But even if the mighty one had not been shaking him so painfully and dreadfully, Shemariah could not have made his story clear in the language of the Christians, which it was all that he could do to understand, and hardly spoke at all. His heart was fluttering wildly; he felt it inside his chest like an intolerably heavy weight that did not, however, hang still but flew madly about. His breath gave out, his mouth fell open, his tongue lolled out; he was panting for air, and as he drew it in and sent it out at once in shallow gasps, shrill, croaking little sighs burst out of him. His whole face pained him, as though ten thousand white-hot needles were being stuck into it.

"Let me die!" he tried to say, but could not.

Through the film that clouded his eyes he could see the face of his tormentor, now enormous, like a huge disk, now tiny as a hazel-nut, and both within the space of a single second. At last he uttered a shrill, ear-splitting scream, torn from the depths of his being. Some soldiers came running up. They saw Shemariah fall to the ground unconscious, and Colonel Tarabas stand over him a while with a lost air. In either hand he held a clump of red beard, and he was smiling. His eyes looked out into a vague distance, and at last he thrust his hands into his pockets, turned round, and went away.

20

TOWARDS six o'clock Colonel Tarabas woke up.
He looked through the uncurtained window and saw
that the stars were out. He thought it must be very
late. He realized that he was in a strange room, and
remembered then that he had come home in the afternoon, come back to the inn, and that the servant Fedya
had given him another room because the dead sergeant-
major Kontsev had lain in his old one. And it came
back to Tarabas that at twelve o'clock midday they
were to have buried Kontsev and the others. It was the
late grandfather's room that he was to have had, therefore this must be it, the room in which the grandfather
of the Jew Kristianpoller had lived, and in which he
had probably also died.

It was not dark. The objects in the room were all
clearly distinguishable in the blue shimmer of the
night. Tarabas sat up. He noticed that he was lying on
the bed in his boots and coat, and with his belt and
shoulder-straps still on. He looked about the room. He
saw a heating-stove, a chest of drawers, a mirror, a
cupboard, bare white-washed walls. One picture only
hung on the wall to the left of the bed. Tarabas got up,

the closer to examine it. It portrayed a broad face surrounded by a fan-like beard. The colonel took a step back. He put his hands into his pockets to get his match-box. They met something hairy and sticky.

He withdrew them instantly. Candle and matches were on the night-table beside the bed. Tarabas lit the candle. He lifted it up to the picture and read the inscription. It said: "Moses Montefiore."

It was a cheap photo-engraving; in hundreds of copies it may be seen in many Jewish homes in the eastern European countries.

The name conveyed nothing to Tarabas. But the beard upset him extraordinarily. He put his hands into his pockets once again and brought out two sticky, matted bunches of red human hair. He threw them on the floor with loathing, then bent down at once and picked them up again. He regarded them a while on his open palm, and put them back into his pockets. This done, he lifted up the candle again and held it close up to the picture, studying the face of Montefiore feature by feature. The picture hung behind glass in a thin, black frame. On his head Montefiore wore a little round skull-cap, precisely like the inn-keeper Kristianpoller. The broad, white face fringed with the fan of thick white hair, reminded one of a benign moon shining through soft clouds on a summer night. The dark and heavy-lidded eyes were fixed upon some definite but unknown distance.

Tarabas put the candle down again upon the night-table, and began to walk up and down the room. He avoided looking at the picture again. But soon he felt distinctly that this Montefiore, whoever he might be, was watching him attentively from the wall. He took the picture down from its nail, turned it round and put it on the chest-of-drawers with its face to the wall. The back of the frame consisted of a thin bare sheet of wood, kept in place at the corners by little nails.

Now Tarabas believed that he could go on walking up and down in peace. But he was mistaken. True, he had turned Montefiore's eyes away, but in his stead there came the red-haired man whose beard he still had in his pockets; there he was in the room as large as life, and as surely as Tarabas himself was there. Tarabas heard again the little, piping cries which the Jew uttered as he was being shaken to and fro, and then the last shrill scream.

Once more Tarabas pulled the matted bunch of hair out of his pocket. He stood looking at it for a long time with dull eyes.

Suddenly he said: "She was right!

"She was right," he repeated—and resumed his pacing up and down the room. "She was right—I am a murderer."

It seemed to him in that moment as though he had shouldered an infinitely heavy burden, but as though at the same time he had been delivered of another, un-

speakably more oppressive still. His state was that of a
man who, with a load at his feet which he has been
condemned countless years ago to lift, knows that he
has become laden with it at last, but without conscious
action on his own part—as though it had put itself alive
upon his back. He bent beneath its weight. He took the
candle in his hand. And as though the door of the
room were not high enough to let him through with
his new load, he put down his head to clear it as he
went. He descended the narrow, creaking stairs, carefully lighting every step. From the parlour the voices
of his fellow-officers came towards him. He entered
with the lighted candle in his hand. He put it down
on the bar-counter. The clock showed seven. He realized that it was only seven o'clock in the evening. He
greeted the officers shortly. They had gathered there
for supper. To Fedya he said in a low voice:

"I want to go down into the cellar to Kristianpoller."

They went down into the cellar. On the last step
Tarabas called out: "It's I—Tarabas!"

Kristianpoller prised up the flagstone with the point
of the iron bar; Fedya pulled it open by the hook.

"Yes, Your Excellency," said Kristianpoller.

"I want to talk to you," said Tarabas. "We can stay
here. Send Fedya away."

When they were alone, Tarabas began.

"Who is that Moses Montefiore of yours?"

"That," answered Kristianpoller, "was a Jew in England. He was the first Jewish mayor of London. When he was invited to dinner with the Queen, they used to cook a special meal for him, just for himself, prepared according to the laws of the Jewish religion. He was a great scholar and a pious Jew."

"Look here," said Tarabas, and pulled the red bunch of beard out of his pocket. "Look here, Kristianpoller, and don't misunderstand me. I hurt a Jew yesterday—very badly."

"Yes, I know, Your Excellency," replied Kristianpoller. "There are a good many here who know my hiding-place. And the Jews come out of their houses just the same. One of them has been here. He told me about it. You pulled Shemariah's beard out."

"I'll send one of my men with you," said Tarabas. "Go and bring that Shemariah to me. I'll wait here till you get back."

They went up the stair. "Guard here!" called Tarabas. The soldier accompanied Kristianpoller into the street.

But in a few minutes the inn-keeper had returned alone.

"He's nowhere to be found," he said. "Your Excellency must know," he added, "he was simple. Not quite right in his mind. It was his son's doing. . . ."

"I know his son," said Tarabas.

"They tell me that he's run away into the woods."

"I'll go and find him," said Tarabas.

They were silent for a long time. They were in the upper story of the cellar, each with a little brandy keg for a seat. On a third one stood the candle. Its light flickered. On the damp, cracked walls the shadows of the two men flitted up and down. Colonel Tarabas seemed to be thinking deeply. Kristianpoller waited.

At last Tarabas spoke. "Listen, Kristianpoller," he said. "Go upstairs and bring me one of your own suits. I'd like to borrow it for a while."

"Certainly. I'll go at once," said the Jew.

"Roll it up into a bundle," Tarabas called after him.

When Kristianpoller returned to the cellar with the bundle, Tarabas said to him: "Thanks, my friend. I'm going to disappear now for a day or two; but I don't want anyone to know."

And he left the cellar.

21

THE priest rose. For the hours he kept, it was late at night and time to go to bed.

"I have come on a personal matter," said Tarabas, still on the threshold. The oil-lamp hung low over the table; its wide shade spread deep shadow over the upper half of the four bare walls. The feeble sight of the old man could not at first distinguish his visitor's face. He stood there in a helpless attitude. His bony aged head, too, stood in the darkness above the lamp-shade, and the light, falling on his old soutane with the innumerable stuff-covered buttons, showed up their shining greasiness more clearly than by day. When he at last recognized Tarabas, the old man came a few hasty little steps towards him.

"Come in, please, and be seated," he said.

Tarabas came over to the table, but did not sit down. The darkness cast by the lamp-shade was what he needed. When he spoke, it was as though he talked into space, not to the priest before him. He pulled the bunch of beard out of his pocket, held it tightly in his hand, and said: "This is the beard of a poor Jew. I pulled it out today." And as though this were an official inquiry in which he was called upon to give all the details he knew, he added:

"His name is Shemariah, and he's got red hair. I sent someone to look for him, but he has disappeared. They say his mind's been turned, and that he has run away into the woods round about. I want to go and look for him myself. What shall I do? Am I to blame that he has gone mad? I wish I'd killed him—that would have been better than this. Yes," Tarabas went on in a toneless voice, "I'd far rather have killed him. I've done in a lot of men in my time, and they didn't worry me afterwards. I was a soldier."

In all his long life, the priest of Koropta had never heard a speech like this. He knew many people, this old man—farmers, their maid-servants, their menservants. He was seventy-six years old, and thirty of these he had lived in Koropta. Before that he had been in other little towns. To countless men and women he had been father-confessor, and all of them had poured much the same sins into his ears. One had beaten his father, who had become ancient and helpless, in the hope that he might die of the effects. Women had deceived their husbands. A thirteen-year-old boy had slept with a sixteen-year-old girl and begotten a boy. The mother had strangled the new-born infant. These were all extraordinary events, and, if the old priest ever took stock of his knowledge of the world and of mankind, these cases seemed to him the most hideous conceivable

examples of what human beings may be brought to by
the abysmal temptations of the devil. Now, listening to
Tarabas, he was rather astonished than appalled.

"Please do sit down," said the old man, for the standing had tired him as much as the remarkable recital
itself. Tarabas sat down.

"Well, now," began the priest, trying to get the matter clear in his own mind, too, "let us try and repeat
what you have said, Colonel. You have torn out the
beard of a Jew unknown to you, named Shemariah.
And what do you mean to do about it? I know this
Shemariah; I've known him for thirty years. He had a
son who became a revolutionist, and he turned him out
of his home. He's a dangerous-looking man, but quite
harmless really, and not altogether right in his mind.
Well, Colonel, what can I do for you?"

"I have not come for practical advice," said Tarabas,
and looked down at the yellow, cracked linoleum with
which the priest's table was covered. "I want to atone!"

They were silent for a long time.

"Colonel," said the priest, "I had better not have
heard this, and will act as though I had not. You may
go now, Colonel, if you would rather—for I have nothing to advise you. Is it spiritual consolation that you
desire? May God forgive you, then! I will pray for you.
You have hurt a poor, foolish Jew. Many of you have
done the same, Colonel. And many more will do
so. . . ."

"I am worse than a murderer," said Tarabas. "And have been for years and years, but I only see it clearly now. I'll atone for everything. I promise you. I shall put off all my murderous splendour and try to make atonement. When I came here, I still had a last, stupid hope—a sinful hope—that you might forgive me, and give me absolution. How could I have thought such a thing!"

"Go now, Colonel, please!" said the priest. "It seems to me that you will find the right way. Go, my son!"

On that same night he rode to the capital. He arrived in the early morning. He inquired where General Lakubeit lived and rode to the house. He tied up his horse and sat down outside the front door to wait until Lakubeit was up.

The general's adjutant, the elegant lieutenant, saw Colonel Tarabas go into the general's room, and leave it again after fifteen minutes. It was remarkable that the colonel had a parcel with him, which he would not allow to leave his hands. As to what took place between the colonel and Lakubeit, the adjutant could not, unfortunately, give any information for the entertainment of the inquisitive officers waiting in the ante-room for an audience.

The officers saluted Tarabas as he passed out. He beckoned the adjutant to him and said:

"I've left my horse outside. I'll be sending for it in a

few days' time. Have it looked after in the meantime,
please."

Tarabas left the house, stood a while still outside the
door, decided to go to the left, and took the broad
street straight through the west of the town until he
reached the fields beyond. He sat down on the edge of
the road, undid his bundle, took off his uniform and
put on Kristianpoller's civilian clothes, went through
the pockets of his uniform, took out nothing but a
knife and Shemariah's beard, folded the garments
neatly, took a last look at them, and then began to
walk along the straight highway that seemed to flow
into the far, far distance and lose itself in the pale
horizon.

22

MANY tramps roam on the highroads of the eastern countries. They can live on the compassion of their fellow-men. The roads are bad, and very tiring to the feet; the huts are poor and mean, and there is little room in them, but the hearts of the people are good, the bread is black and wholesome, and the doors open more readily. Even today despite the great war and the great revolution, although machines have started on their steel, precise, uncanny march towards the east of Europe, the people are still kind to the misery of strangers. There even the fools and imbeciles have a quicker and a better grasp of their neighbours' need than the wise ones and the clever ones elsewhere. Asphalt has not yet covered all the highways. The laws and the caprices of the weather, the seasons, and the earth still change and determine the aspect and condition of the roads. In the little huts, that cling so close against the bosom of the earth, the people in them are as near to it as to the sky. Yes, there the sky itself comes down to earth and to the people, whereas in other places where the houses reach up towards it, it seems to draw away from them ever farther and ever higher.

Great distances apart and scattered over all the land lie
the villages. The little towns are rare, the large towns
rarer, but the highroads and the by-ways are alive.
Many people come and go upon them permanently.
Their freedom and their poverty are loving sisters. This
one must be a wanderer because he has no home; that
one because he can find no rest; a third, because he will
not rest, or because he has taken a vow to eschew repose; a fourth, because the road and the unknown
houses of strangers are what he loves. One knows that
in the eastern countries now, as in the west, they have
begun to campaign against the beggar and the tramp.
It is as though the unrest of the factories and machines, the windiness of dwellers on the sixth floor,
the deceptively settled ones in their here-today and
gone-tomorrow instability, can no longer bear the
thought of the honest, calm, unceasing movement of
the good and aimless wanderers. Where are you going
to? What are you going to do when you get there?
Why did you take to the road? How do you come to
lead a life of your own, when we can all endure a common life? Are you better? Are you different?

Of those whom the former Colonel Nicholas Tarabas met on his wanderings here and there, were many
who put this kind of question to him. He gave no answers. Kristianpoller's clothes had long since gone to
rags. His boots were torn. Tarabas still wore his soldier's great-coat. He had taken off the epaulettes and

put them in a pocket. Sometimes he put his hand into
his pocket to feel them, sometimes he took them out
and looked at them. The tarnished silver was yellow
now, old toys. He put them back again into the pocket.
He had taken the cockade off his cap. It sat upon his
shaggy, unshorn mane of hair like a little wheel, far
too small. It had lost its pretty grey colour. It shimmered white in some places, also greyish, yellow, and
green. Round his neck, underneath his shirt, the former
colonel wore two little twin bags. In one were bank-
notes and coins. In the other he kept an object which
he would not have parted with if his life and hope of
heaven had depended on his doing so.

Whenever he came upon a shrine or crucifix along
the way, he knelt down and prayed long prayers before
it. He prayed with fervour, although he thought he
had nothing left to implore. He was content, serene,
and happy in spirit. He went to great pains to find
troubles and suffering and harsh treatment. But people
were too good to him. Seldom was he refused a bowl of
soup, a piece of bread, a shelter for the night. Did this
occur, however, he answered with a blessing. He even
had a gentle word for dogs who came and barked at
him or tried to bite him. And if he came where they
said to him: "Go away, we've nothing for ourselves,"
then Tarabas would answer: "God's blessing be on
you! May He give you everything you need."

Only the first week had been hard.

The lovely autumn had changed overnight to harshest winter. First the fierce rains had come; the drops had frozen singly as they fell and struck the body and face like grains of ice. Then they had become monstrous hail-stones which had swept down in a sloping, savage wall. Tarabas had welcomed the first snow, the winter's good and gentle son. The roads became soft and bottomless. The snow melted. One longed for a solid, bitter frost. One day it came, in company with its brother, the steady, calmly moving wind from out of the north, which comes like a sword, flat, broad, and whetted to a fearful keenness. It cuts through armour. No garment can resist it. One puts one's hands deep into one's pockets. But the north wind blows through stuff as though it were tissue-paper. Under its breath the earth is frozen instantly, and sends its own icy breath up into the air. The wanderer grows light—yes, lighter than down; the wind can blow him clean away like the spat-out shell of a pumpkin-seed. The nearest village is far away, farther than usual. No living thing but has crept away into hiding. Even the ravens and the crows, the birds of coldest winter, the heralds of death itself, are dumb. And on either side of the frozen road, to right and left of the wanderer, spreads the plain; as far as the eye can see lie fields and meadows, covered with a thin, transparent, brittle skin of whitish ice.

In the country where the story of our Nicholas Tara-

bas took place, there was a guild of beggars and tramps.
A well-tried, good community of the homeless, with
its own customs, its own laws and now and then its
own jurisdiction, its own symbols, and its own speech.
These beggars are the proprietors of certain houses, too:
sheds, abandoned shepherds' huts, partially burnt-out
houses, forgotten railway cars, certain caves they know
of. Whoever has spent four weeks on the road has
learnt, taught by mankind's two greatest teachers, poverty and solitude, to read the secret symbols which announce a shelter in the neighbourhood. Here lies a
piece of string, there a rag torn from a handkerchief,
yonder a charred twig. Here, in a declivity at the roadside, one comes upon the remains of a fire. There, underneath the varnish of the frost, the print of human
footsteps may be seen, all going one way and in one
direction. The frost cuts into the flesh, and whets the
wits as well.

Tarabas learnt to know the signs that promise
warmth and safety. The war had left a great deal of
useful material lying about the countryside, corrugated
iron and sheet-iron, wood, broken motor-cars, train-cars
left astray on narrow, improvised rails, tumble-down
barracks, half-burnt cottages, abandoned trenches, well
reinforced with cement. In a land where war has destroyed the possessions of the settled ones, the wanderers
on the highways are well off.

When the former Colonel Tarabas entered one of

these shelters, he felt that he was being rewarded far
beyond his merits. And he almost regretted having
come there. Yes, sometimes it happened that he had
hardly arrived and let the warmth envelop him when
he had got up and was gone again, having stayed there
only a few moments. He was not entitled to enjoy more
warmth and shelter than were absolutely needed to
keep life in him. For he enjoyed his torments, and
wished to prolong them if he could.

And so he went out again into the snow and ice and
darkness. If another wanderer, making for the refuge,
met him on the way and asked him whither he was
bound, Tarabas would answer that he must reach a
certain destination that day—that night.

One evening he came to one of these asylums, and
found someone else already there. It was a damaged
second-class train-carriage standing on the disused rails
of an old cross-country railway. The windows of the
compartments were broken and had been replaced with
boards and cardboard. The doors between the corridor
and the compartments would not shut. The leather up-
holstery of the seats had long since been cut away. The
hard grey horse-hair sprouted in clumps out of the
seats. Through chinks and apertures the wind blew
mercilessly without a pause. Tarabas went into the first
compartment. A second-class carriage, such as Tarabas
had travelled in a thousand times in other days. He was
very tired and went to sleep immediately. He carried

with him into sleep the memory of the day when, as a "special courier of the Tsar on a secret mission," he had come back to his home. "Guard!" he had called, "I want some tea!" And: "Guard! Fetch me some grapes!"—Room, room the people in the corridor had made for the special courier of the Tsar. Ah, what a man Nicholas Tarabas had been! What were his old guard doing without Tarabas? Look, said Tarabas to himself, a man can live with all that power and magnificence, and be a mighty Tarabas, and think the world will be a different place the day he ceases to be there. But now I've left the world—and it has not changed its looks in the very least. We're nothing to the world one way or the other, none of us, not even such a man of power as I was!

Tarabas slept for two hours, then awoke. He opened his eyes and saw another figure in the darkness, an aged tramp. His white hair flowed over the collar of his dark coat, and his beard almost met the rope around his waist.

"You must be one of the Seven Sleepers," said the old man. "Here I've been standing for a quarter of an hour, coughing and spitting, and not a thing did you hear. I heard you when you came, though, but you never even noticed that someone else was living in this car. You're young still. I'll bet it's not long since you took to the road!"

"How do you know that?" asked Tarabas, and sat up.

"Because the first thing even a half-way experienced tramp does is to go through every place he comes into. How easily you might find something useful! A coin, tobacco, a candle, a piece of bread, or even a gendarme! Those queer fellows have a way of hiding in our places and waiting till the likes of us arrive, and then they want to see our papers. . . . But I'm all right, I've got mine," he added after a pause. "I could show them to you if we had a light."

"Here's a candle," said Tarabas.

"I can't light it," answered the old man. "You must do it yourself."

Tarabas lit the candle-end and stuck it on the narrow window-sill.

"Why wouldn't you light it?" he asked, looking at the old wanderer with a touch of envy, because he was so much older and looked so much more ravaged by suffering than Tarabas. Ah, this was a general in the army of the wretched! Tarabas was but a lieutenant still.

"This is Friday night," said the other. "I am a Jew, and we are not allowed to make a fire on the Sabbath."

"How is it that you aren't in a warm house tonight?" asked Tarabas, and now his envy filled him to the brim, as formerly only his rages could. "All other Jews eat and sleep in their houses when the Sabbath comes. I have never met a Jewish beggar before on Friday night or Saturday."

"Well, you see," said the aged Jew, sitting down on the seat opposite Tarabas, "with me it's different. I was a respected man in my community. I celebrated every Sabbath as God commands. But many other things that He commands, I did not do. It's eight years now since I have been a wanderer like this. I was on the road all the years of the war. And those were by no means the worst. I've been a long way round, and seen many parts of Russia. And sometimes I was very close to the front. Close to the troops there was always something interesting going on, and always something to spare for a beggar."

"But why have you given up observing your Sabbath?" asked Tarabas.

The old man passed his hand through his beard, leaned forward to take a nearer look at Tarabas, and said:

"Move a bit nearer to the light, so that I can get a look at you."

Tarabas did so.

"Good!" said the old Jew. "I think you're one that I can tell my story to. To be frank, I like telling it. But there are some folk you can talk to, and all they say is 'Yes, yes' or 'Is that so?' or else they only smile, or are altogether deaf and dumb and say nothing at all. They only turn over and begin to snore at you. Now, heaven knows, I'm not a vain man, and I don't want applause—on the contrary, I want others to know me as I am, exactly as I am. And unless they take my whole nature into consideration, it's no use my telling them my tale at all."

"Quite right," said Tarabas. "I understand."

"Well, I'll tell you," continued the Jew—and to Tarabas's astonishment he spoke the language of the country with perfect fluency, not like the other Jews. "I'll tell you to begin with that I was a very rich man once. My name is Samuel Yedliner. And everybody in this country for miles around knows me. But I don't advise you to mention me to anyone, for they'll only curse you if you say my name. Remember that. Especially if you should ever come to Koropta. That's where I used to live."

"Koropta?" asked Tarabas.

"Yes. Do you know it?"

"Slightly," said Tarabas.

"Yes," said the aged Yedliner. "I had a house there, as big as the Koropta inn, Kristianpoller's inn. I had a beautiful wife, strong, and buxom; and two sons. I traded in timber, I must tell you, and made a pile of money. You sell a lot of wood when the winter's hard, like this one now, for instance. I wasn't the only timber-merchant in the place; but I was the smartest of them all. It's this way: in spring, when no one ever thinks that there will ever be a winter, I go to the owner of the big estate and look at his forest, and have this tree marked, and that one, and pay him something on

account. Then I have my trees cut down. I don't rely
on the owner—let him cut down what he likes. I have
my own wood-cutters. The trees are delivered in my
yard. I let them lie out of doors when it's wet, and
when it's dry I cover them over. That's how you bring
up the weight. For my one great principle was sale by
weight, and as far as possible already sawn and chopped
up small. You see?—Why should the people have men
come and chop up their logs, and pay them extra for
it? If they buy by the cord or by the foot they only
have to get the trees sawed up for them. No, that's not
my way. I sell wood ready for use, and by weight. Now
that was an absolutely original method in our part of
the country."

The old man broke off. Perhaps he reflected that this
passion which he still could feel for his abandoned
calling was no longer right or proper. He interrupted
his description.

"Well, it was like that—more or less. It doesn't matter any more. At any rate, I was a rich man. I had
money in the house and in the bank. I had one son at
the university. I sent my wife abroad every year, to
Austria, to Franzensbad, because the doctor said she
must have some internal trouble to account for the
pains in her back, that he could find no reason for. But
the devil pinched me. All summer long I earned no
money, and I had no patience to wait until the autumn
came. Besides, sometimes the autumns were fine and

dry and very late, and no one thought about the winter
—and my wood got lighter and lighter. That was pretty
galling. Then that Yurych came to me one day, and
made me a proposal. . . ."

Yedliner paused, sighed, and then went on.

"And from that day on, I was a well-paid spy in the
service of the police. To begin with I only denounced
people that I knew something positive against; but then
I went on to others where I could only guess; and
finally, anyone I had a personal grudge against I simply
reported. I developed a tremendous imagination, and
I was good at putting two and two together. They believed me without question. Once or twice I had luck;
it turned out that everything I said was true, although
I had simply gone on guess-work. But then one day
Yurych went to Kristianpoller's bar and got drunk, and
said that I was earning a great deal more money than
he himself.

"Well, I don't want to bore you. To make a long
story short, they fetched me out one night. Two strong
Jewish butchers and the inn-keeper Kristianpoller,
who's no weakling either, beat me half to death. They
forced me to leave my home and the town. My wife
wouldn't go with me. My sons spat at me. The rabbi
called a Jewish court together; three very learned men
sat in it. I saw what I'd done—at least twenty Jews from
Koropta and round about were in prison on my account. And at least ten of them were innocent. And I

swore to the Jews of Koropta that I would give up everything and go away. And that I would join the beggars of the country. And to myself I vowed and resolved that I would never again spend Sabbath in a Jewish house.

"That's why I'm here. And that is my story."

"And I," said Tarabas, "got into a fury with one of your people, and pulled out his beard."

They sat there facing each other. The stump of candle on the window-sill had gone out long ago.

When the morning came, an icy morning—its red and fiery dawn announced another snowstorm—they left the train-carriage, shook each other's hand, and went their separate ways, in different directions.

23

ON that forenoon Tarabas came to the market-village of Turka. Old Yedliner's story had given him a desire to saw up tree-trunks and chop them into logs.

Therefore he went in Turka from one house to another, asking if there was wood to chop. He found what he was looking for, half a cord of oak to be made small.

"What do you want for your work?" asked the owner of the wood.

"I shall be satisfied with any wage," Tarabas answered.

"Very well," said the master of the house.

He was a well-to-do man, a horse-dealer. He brought Tarabas into the yard and showed him where the wood was, brought axe and saw out of the shed and the wooden sawhorse which the people here call the "scissors." Before he went into the yard, the horse-dealer had put on a fur coat lined with beaver, with a collar of beautiful curly astrakhan. His face was ruddy and smooth with good nourishment, his legs were encased in fur-lined high boots, he held his hands in his warm pockets. Tarabas, on the other hand, frozen in his military coat, blew upon his numb hands, and tried to cover first his right and then his left ear with the inadequate cap, for the frost was pricking both with innumerable pins and needles. The horse-dealer looked at him suspiciously. Tarabas's face was covered with an unkempt blond beard which began at the cheekbones and bushed out over the collar of his coat. Other tramps, at least so long as they were still young, like this one here, went to the trouble of shaving once a fortnight or so. This one surely has something to hide, reflected the horse-dealer. What tell-tale murderous or thievish feature is he hiding underneath that beard? He might take the axe and saw, and simply make off with them! The cautious man decided that he would keep an eye on this stranger while he worked.

Now Tarabas, faced with the task of chopping wood for the first time in his life, set about it so unskilfully that the horse-dealer's suspicions were redoubled.

"Listen here," he said, and grasped Tarabas by a button of his coat. "By the looks of it, you've never done any work before?"

Tarabas nodded.

"You're a convict or a criminal of some kind, eh? And you think I'm going to leave you alone in my yard? So that you can take a good look round, and come back in the night and rob me? You can't fool me,

my man, and I'm not afraid of you either. I was in the
trenches three years—I was in eight big drives. Do you
know what that means, eh?"

Tarabas only nodded.

The horse-dealer took away the axe and saw, and
said: "Be off now, before I hand you over to the police.
And don't let me see your face round here again."

"God be with you, sir!" said Tarabas, and went
slowly out of the yard.

The horse-dealer looked after him. He was warm
and cosy in his beaver coat. He felt the frost in his
ruddy face as no more than a pleasant device of heaven
—perhaps designed for that special purpose—to encourage a good appetite in house-owners and horse-
dealers. Besides, it pleased him that he had had the
cleverness to see through that suspicious fellow so
promptly, and put the fear of God into him with his
strong right hand. In addition to which he had been
given the opportunity to mention his eight big drives
once again. And finally it occurred to him that the
tramp had asked for no wages. He would most likely
have been satisfied with a bowl of soup in payment of
his work. These considerations had a softening effect
upon the horse-dealer. And he called Tarabas back before he had reached the outside gate.

"I'll give you another trial," he said, "because I've
got a kind heart. How much do you want for your
work?"

"I'll be content with anything you give me," Tarabas repeated.

He began to saw the trunk which he had laid with such evidently unpractised hands upon the stand before. He worked diligently, under his employer's eye, and as he worked he felt the strength increasing in his muscles. He was in haste to be done, so that he might get away from the horse-dealer's mistrustful eyes. But the man was coming to like Tarabas more and more. He was also not a little afraid of the stranger's undeniably great strength. Also one could admit to a certain curiosity when one found oneself confronted with so remarkable a man. Therefore the master of the house said: "Come inside; you'd better have a drink to warm you up a bit!"

For the first time since many a long day Tarabas drank a glass of spirits. It was a good, strong liquor, clean and clear, greenly tinged and bitterly spiced with many different herbs which could be seen swimming about in the bottom of the massive, wide-bellied bottle like seaweed in an aquarium. They were good, reliable household health-herbs, such as Tarabas's old father used to mix with the liquor at home. It burnt, a brief, quick fire in the throat, immediately extinguished, to change into a comforting and spacious warmth lower down. It went into the limbs, then to the head.

Tarabas stood there, the little glass in one hand, his

cap in the other. His eyes betrayed such appreciation and contentment that his host, at once flattered and stirred to pity, poured him out another. Tarabas tossed it off at a single draught. His limbs grew limp, his mind confused. He wished he might sit down, but did not dare. Suddenly he was conscious of hunger, an immense hunger; it seemed to him that he could feel with his hands the absolutely void, immeasurable cavern of his stomach. His heart contracted. His mouth gaped open. For an instant which seemed to him eternity, he groped in emptiness with both his hands, caught at a chair-back and fell with a great noise to the ground, while the frightened horse-dealer uselessly and helplessly rushed to the door and tore it open. The horse-dealer's wife flew in from the next room. They threw a pail of water over Tarabas. He woke, rose slowly, went over to the stove, wrung the water out of his coat and cap without a word, said then: "God's blessing be on you!" and left the house.

For the first time the lightning of disease had struck him. And already he felt the first touch of death.

24

THIS year the wanderers on the highroads were impatient for the spring. It was a hard winter. It could last a long while yet, before it decided to go from the land. It had struck a hundred thousand fine, inextricably branching roots of ice into the ground everywhere. Deep underneath the earth and high over it the winter had had its dwelling. The seed was dead below, the grass and bushes dead above the ground. Even the sap in the trees at the edge of the roads and in the forests seemed to be petrified for ever. Very slowly the snow began to melt in the ploughland and the meadows, and then only in the short midday hours. But in the dark depths, in the ditches along the roadside, it still lay clear and stiff over a thick crust of ice.

It was the middle of March, and icicles were still hanging from the roofs; they melted for an hour in the brightness of the noonday sunshine. In the afternoon, when the dusk fell again, they congealed to spears once more, immovable, sharp, and brilliant. Upon the floor of the forests everything was still asleep. And in the crests of the trees no bird's voice was to be heard. The sky abode immaculate in icy cobalt-blue. The birds of spring would not venture into that dead clarity.

The new laws of the new state were no less inimical to the wanderers than was the winter. In a new state order must reign. It must not be said of it that it is barbarian, still less a "musical comedy" affair. The statesmen of the new country have studied laws and legislation at ancient universities. The new engineers have studied at the old schools of technology. And the newest noiseless, dependable, precise machines are coming on silent, dangerous wheels into the new country. Civilization's most dangerous beasts of prey, the great rolls of paper on which the daily press is printed, glide into the new great presses, unroll themselves independently of human agency, cover themselves with politics and art and science and literature, arrange themselves in columns, fold themselves, and flutter out into the little towns and villages. They fly into houses, cottages, and huts. And thus the newest state has reached completion. Upon its highways there are more gendarmes than tramps. Every beggar must possess a paper, for all the world as though he were a person owning money. And whoever does own money takes it to the banks. In the capital there is a stock exchange.

Tarabas was waiting for the twenty-first of March, when he would go into the capital. That was the date which General Lakubeit had set for him. Tarabas still had five days' time. He remembered his last talk with Lakubeit. The little man had not had much time to

spare. He urged Tarabas to be as quick with his story
as he could.

"I understand! I understand!" he had said. "Just go
on, and tell me everything." And when Tarabas had
told it all, Lakubeit said: "Good. Nobody shall know
anything about you. Not even your father. You can try
until the twentieth of March next year, and see whether
you can stand that life. Then write to me. From the
twenty-first of March on," Lakubeit had said, "I shall
see that you receive your pension monthly."

"Good-bye," Tarabas had said. And without waiting
for an answer, ignoring Lakubeit's outstretched hand,
he had gone away. That was more than four months
ago! Sometimes Tarabas longed to meet somebody who
had known him in the past and would recognize him
again in spite of everything. Surely there could hardly
be a more voluptuous manner of humiliating oneself
than that! In his sinful moments, that is, in the moments which he called sinful, Tarabas would look back
over the short but eventful way upon which he had acquired the distinctions and insignia of poverty with the
self-admiration with which others, who have attained
to fame or riches after poor or obscure beginnings, are
wont to look back on their "career." Nor could he quite
overcome a certain vanity concerning his appearance.
Sometimes he would stand before his own reflection in
a shop window, and look at himself with grim and
spiteful satisfaction. Immersed in contemplation of his

image, he would stand there until he had resumed before his mind's eye his appearance of the past, his uniform, his tall boots. And then he would find bitter joy in pulling it to pieces, bit by bit; watching the shaven, powdered cheeks cover themselves with the unkempt beard, observing how the upright back bent over in a gentle curve.

"Yes, that's you, the real Tarabas!" he would say then to himself. "Years ago when you associated with the revolutionists, the mark was on your forehead already. Later, when you were a loafer about the New York streets you were a good-for-nothing. Your father saw through you, Nicholas Tarabas! You spat at him— that was your farewell to your father! The red-haired soldier that had no God, he knew you for what you were, so did the clever Lakubeit. Many people, Tarabas, have known that you deceived others and yourself as well. It wasn't your real rank that you paraded with all that mightiness; no, your uniform was a masquerade, and nothing else. I like you as you are now, Tarabas!"

In this wise Tarabas spoke to himself now and then, in the crowded, narrow streets of some town, and the people laughed at him. They took him for one not altogether in his right senses. He would then hurry away, lest they call the police. He remembered the three policemen in New York whom he had let go by, when he was still the superstitious coward Tarabas. I am

atoning for that as well, he told himself with quiet joy.
I should like to stop them myself and let them take me
away with all the street-urchins looking on. But they
would find out who I am.

Always, when he held such soliloquies as these, and
when old memories raced through his brain and away
from him, try as he might to detain them, he felt himself burning and freezing in turns. It was fever. Often
this fever caught him and put him in an ague. It began
to consume his powerful body. It established itself in
his face. It dug hollows in his bearded cheeks. Sometimes his feet swelled up, so that he could hardly walk.
Many a night when he found a shelter where one
might undress, he found that he could remove his
boots only with a great effort. His brethren of the road,
watching him, inspected his swollen limbs with expert
eyes and prescribed all kinds of remedies: hayflower
baths and ribwort-tea; diuretic herbs of all kinds, goat's
beard and wild masterwort and wild hart's wort. They
praised the virtues of bog-bean, rosemary, and wild
succory. His ailments inspired many nightly debates.
There were always some who, in the course of their
chequered lives, had had exactly the same complaints.
But no sooner had he fallen asleep than they nudged
one another and showed by signs that they did not give
him much longer to live. They made a sign of the
cross over the sleeper, and then composed themselves
to sleep, contented with their lot. For even the sons of

wretchedness loved their lives, and clung with ardour
to this earth which they knew so well, its beauty and
its cruelty; and they rejoiced in their good health when
they saw another limping towards death. As for Tarabas, he worried more over his torn boots than over his
swollen feet. Never mind if clothes hang in rags, boots
must be whole! They are the wanderer's tools. There
may be long, long roads before you, Tarabas!

Sometimes he had to stop in the middle of the road
and sit down. His heart raced violently. His hands
shook. Before his eyes a grey mist formed, making
even the nearest objects impossible to distinguish. The
single trees on the opposite side of the road dissolved
into a dense and endless procession of trunks and
branches, an indistinct but impenetrable wall of trees.
They hid the sky. One sat in the midst of open country
and it was as though one were imprisoned in an airless
room. Heavy weights pressed upon one's chest and
shoulders. Tarabas coughed and spat. Slowly then the
cloud before his eyes dispersed. The trees along the
roadside opposite parted and grew distinct again. The
world resumed its normal aspect. Tarabas could go on.

The capital was still two hours' walk away. A peasant driving his milk to town stopped and beckoned to
him to get up beside him into the cart.

"I've got milk enough and to spare, praise be to
God," the man said as they drove along. "Have some,
if you're thirsty."

Since his childhood Tarabas had not tasted milk. Now, as he lifted a snow-white bottle to his lips, surrounded by full and rattling cans in which the milk could be heard splashing richly, his heart was deeply stirred. He seemed to realize all at once the blessing, yes, the miracle, of milk, so white, so full of goodness, the most innocent fluid in all the world. Milk—such an everyday and obvious thing! Nobody stops to think that it is wonderful. It has its source in mothers; in them the warm, red blood is transformed into cool, white milk, the first sustenance of men and animals, the white and flowing greeting of the earth to all its new-born children.

"You know," said Tarabas to the dairy-farmer, "it's a wonderful thing this, that you're driving in your cart."

"Yes, yes," said the peasant, "it's splendid milk, is mine. In all Kurki—that's my village—you'll not find any like it. I've got five cows; their names are Terepa, Lala, Korova, Dusha, and Luna. Dusha's the best. She's a sweet one, she is! You ought to see her, only. You'd love her at once. She gives the best milk of all. There's a brown patch on her forehead—the others are all white. But she wouldn't need her brown patch for me to recognize her anywhere. It's her eyes, you know, and her tail—she's got a pretty little tail—and her voice, too. She's like a human being. Just exactly like a human being. We get on fine together, me and Dusha."

Now they had come into the town, and Tarabas got

down. He went to the post-office. It was the general
post-office, a new and splendid building. There was a
young lady presiding over a little stationery stall outside the magnificent entrance; Tarabas bought paper,
an envelope, and a pen of her. Then he entered the
great hall and wrote at a desk to General Lakubeit.

"Your Excellency," he wrote. "This is the day on
which you told me to report. I do so respectfully here-
with. I take the liberty of submitting two requests to
your kind attention: first, that you would be so kind
as to give instructions for my pension to be paid me in
gold or silver, if this is convenient; secondly, that you
will permit me to fetch the money at an hour when
nobody will see me. With your kind permission I shall
receive the answer to this letter here, poste restante. I
remain Your Excellency's most grateful and humble
servant, Nicholas Tarabas, Colonel. Poste restante."

He dispatched the letter. He went on his crippled
feet to the hostel for vagrants, spotless and new and
equipped with all the improvements of its western
models. Here, with many others, he was deloused,
bathed, cleansed, and presented with a bowl of soup.
He was given a number on a tin disk, and a hard straw
mattress chemically cleaned.

Upon this he slept until the following morning.

At the poste restante counter there was a letter for
Nicholas Tarabas addressed in Lakubeit's own hand.

"Dear Colonel Tarabas," he had written. "If you will go today or tomorrow about twelve o'clock midday to the post-office, a young man will meet you there and hand you your pension. You need not fear any indiscretion; for our new army, your old father, and the world you are dead and forgotten. Lakubeit, General."

At twelve o'clock, as most of the counters were closing, the clerks going home and the people leaving the great hall, a young man accosted Tarabas.

"Colonel," said the young man, "please sign this receipt."

Tarabas received eighty golden five-franc pieces.

"I hope you will excuse it," said the young gentleman, "but we could not get it all in gold this time. We hope to do better next month. At this time a month from now, will you please meet me again at this same spot?"

Tarabas went to the city gates, stood there for a moment—and then turned back at once towards the massive entrance of the post-office. In the wide square a few carriages were waiting, a horse or two tied up to the lamp-posts, a few motor-cars. It was the first warm day that spring. The noonday sun flooded the wide, stone, unshaded square with its good warmth. The horses had their heads deep in their nose-bags, eating with happy appetite, and seemed blissfully conscious of the sunshine. Suddenly one of them, harnessed to a light, two-wheeled trap, lifted its head out of the nose-bag and whinnied joyfully. It was a handsome creature. Its coat was silver grey, with big, regular brown patches. Tarabas recognized it instantly, by its neck, by its whinnying call, by the brown patches.

He went into the hall, sat down on a bench and waited. When the dinner-hour was over and the counters began to open again, and the people began to fill the hall, the elder Tarabas also appeared. He had grown very old. He went now supported on two sticks. They were ebony sticks, with silver handles. The old man's mighty moustache fell like an imposing chain across his mouth, parted in the middle and falling down low on either side, silver-white, and the two fine points touched the high snow-white collar. The old Tarabas crossed the hall unsteadily from one end to the other. The lesser folk made way for him. Upon the flagstones each of his dragging steps could be heard, and the dull, almost ghostly tapping of his two sticks with rubber tips. As the old man came to the counter, the clerk thrust his head through the window towards him.

"Good day, sir!" said the clerk.

Tarabas the younger left his bench and approached the counter where his father stood. He saw him hang one of his sticks on the ledge of the counter, pull out his wallet, fumble in it till he found some coupons, and hand these over to the clerk. Then he departed. He almost brushed against his son in passing. But with his eyes fixed on the ground, and without a look around him, he hobbled out of the building.

Nicholas followed him. He stood at the gate and saw a sympathetic stranger help the old man into the trap. Both sticks were propped beside him against the driver's box. He gathered the reins into his hands. The horse set off. And old Tarabas drove home.

Home.

25

ONE day—it was already the end of May—Tarabas felt that the time had come to go back home and see his father and mother and sister once again. Often during his wanderings he had found himself near his native village, but had always made a wide detour round it. He was not yet sufficiently prepared; for it needs much preparation before one is ready to go home again.

Tarabas was cut off from all the world. But he was still afraid to visit the places of his childhood. He did not love his father. He never had loved his father. He could not remember his father's ever having either kissed or beaten him. For old Tarabas was seldom angry, and as seldom was his humour good. He ruled in his household which contained his wife and children, like a king who belonged neither there nor to them. A simple, bare, and iron ritual regulated his days, his evenings, his meals, his conduct, and that of the mother and the children. It seemed as though he had never been a young man. It was as though he had come into the world with his established ritual, a complete time-table of his life and days; that he must have been be-

gotten and born according to special laws, and grown
up according to rules and regulations of extreme rigid-
ity, and contrary to nature. It was most probable that
he had never experienced any form of passion, and
certainly he had never known hardship. His own father's life had ended early, "in an accident," so it was
always said. Nobody knew what manner of accident it
had been. As a boy young Tarabas used to imagine that
his grandfather had been killed out hunting, in a fight
with wolves or bears. For a few years his grandmother
had lived on in her son's house, in the room which was
given to his little sister after the old woman's death had
left it vacant.

His sister—she was ten years old at the time—had
been afraid lest the dead grandmother return. Even in
life she had been a majestic ghost moving through the
house, tall and big, with a broad coif on her head, snow-
white and stiffly starched, her imposing figure en-
veloped in solemn, stiff black silk, a kind of stone silk,
and in her plump and soft white hands she always held
a purple rosary. Without visible reason, and apparently
with the sole purpose of showing that her silent majesty
was still alive, she descended the stair to the kitchen
every day, received the obeisances of the cook and servants with a silent inclination of the head, billowed
across the yard towards the stables, vouchsafed the
groom a cold glance from her big brown eyes, which
stood out from their sockets and were perpetually

moist, and returned the way she had come. At meals
she was enthroned at the head of the table. Father,
mother, and the children approached her and kissed her
soft, muscleless, and doughy hand before the soup was
brought on to the table. In the presence of the grandmother no word was ever spoken. There was no sound
but the imbibing of the soup and the soft clink of
spoons against the dishes. After the soup, when the
meat course arrived, the old woman left the table. She
went to lie down. Nobody knew whether she really
slept, or even rested. During the evening she appeared
again, to depart as before after a quarter of an hour.
Although she never spoke, or interfered in anything
concerning the house or the estate, and was so seldom
to be seen, yet her presence was felt by everyone—except by her son, perhaps—as a burden no less unbear-
able for being never mentioned. The servants hated her
and called her "the shadow-queen." Her eyes, perpetually moist, glittered with malevolence, and her wordless
hauteur aroused those about her to a hatred equally
silent and vindictive. They would gladly have put an
end to the shadow-queen, if the opportunity had offered. The children, too, Nicholas and his sister, hated
the grandmother in her wicked majesty moving within
the folds of heavy stuffs which muffled every sound.
And when she died one day, suddenly and without
warning, and as silently as she had lived, the entire
household breathed again—but only for a while.

Father Tarabas succeeded to his mother's throne, in-
heriting the deathly, icy majesty that had been hers.
Thenceforth it was he who sat at the head of the table.
Thenceforth it was his hand the children kissed before
the meal began. He differed from his mother only in
that he remained after the soup, partaking of the meat
course and dessert with chilly appetite, and only then
departed to lie down. If in former days, while his
mother was still alive, he had now and then, naturally
in her absence, talked a little, and even unbent to an
occasional jest, now, after her death, he seemed to
emanate her entire ponderous sombreness. And they
called him after his mother, "the shadow-king."

His wife submitted to him with unquestioning obedience. She often wept. With her tears she washed away
all the small store of strength with which nature had
endowed her. She was thin and pale. With her peaked
face and sunken chin, her red-rimmed eyes and the
eternal blue apron which covered her whole dress, she
looked like a servant, a kind of privileged cook or
housekeeper. And the kitchen was where she spent
most of her day. Her hard, dry hands, with which she
sometimes stroked her children, shyly, almost timidly,
as though committing some forbidden action, smelt
of onions. When she put them out towards the children, her tears began to flow simultaneously and ir-
resistibly; it was as though she wept at the tenderness
which she bestowed upon the little ones. Nicholas and

his sister began to avoid their mother. Every approach
to her was bound up inevitably with tears and onions.
She frightened them.

And yet it was home. Stronger than the sombre
majesty of the father and the tearful helplessness of the
mother, were the silver magic of the birches, the dark
mystery of the pine wood, the fragrance of potatoes
roasting in autumnal fields, the joyous trilling of larks
in the sky, the wind's monotonous song, the gay regatta
of the clouds in spring, the eerie tales of the maids indoors on winter evenings, the crackling of fresh logs
burning in the stove, the oily, resinous scent that went
out from them, and the ghostly light the snow cast
into the room through the windows, before the lights
were lit. All this was home. The strange, inaccessible
father and the poor, insignificant mother received a
measure of the sentiments which all the rest invoked
so powerfully, and Tarabas gave them part of the love
he felt for all the things which went into the making
of his childhood's landscape. Memories of the strength
and sweetness of that earth cloaked all the strangeness
of his parents in a mantle of reconciliation.

Ah, he was afraid to see his home again! He had
still been too weak! One can part with power, with
war, and with the uniform; with remembrance of
Maria, with the pleasures a man like Tarabas knows in
the arms of women—but from the silver birch trees of

home there is no parting. His old father whom he had
seen upon two crutches, was he near death now?—Was
his mother still alive?—What did his sister look like?—
Had Tarabas a great desire to know these things?—
He did not know that it was not the sight of his infirm
old father which had awakened his nostalgia, but the
sudden whinny of the horse, the brown-spotted grey.
In that voice all his home had called to him.

The following morning—a soft, sad rain was falling,
as it does in spring, mild and full of goodness—Tarabas took the road that leads to Koryla. Towards ten
o'clock he came to where the avenue of birch began,
which led to the house. Yes, the hollows along the
road were still the same, and had been filled with
gravel as he had known it done years ago. Each separate tree was known to Tarabas. If trees had names, he
could have called each one by its own. On either hand
the fields spread out before him. They, too, belonged
to the master of Koryla. These were the fallow fields,
left so as long as anyone could remember; they were
a sign that one was rich enough, and had no need to
plough more land than one had under grain already.
True the incendiary boots of war had trampled this
earth as well; but the earth of the Tarabases produced
in indefatigable freshness new seed, new wild plants,
new grass; it was endowed with a luxuriant, irrespon-
sible fruitfulness, it survived wars, it was stronger than

death. Nicholas Tarabas, too, the last scion of that earth, and to whom it had ceased to belong, even he was proud of it, of this triumphant earth.

But he must go warily. He knew that in the yard behind the house the dogs began to bark as soon as any stranger passed the sixth birch from the house-door. He was at pains to move as quietly as he could. He could no longer manage the long way round, along the willow path between the marshes, to reach the house through the yard and climb the vine-grown wall, as he had done on that other homecoming! Now he shuffled quietly up the six low steps that led to the russet-coloured door of the broad, white-painted house. The knocker hung on a rusty wire at the door; he knocked, timidly, as befits a beggar. He waited.

He waited long. The door was opened. It was a young servant who had opened it; Tarabas had never seen him before.

He said immediately: "The master won't have beggars coming here!"

"I'm looking for work," answered Tarabas. "And I'm very hungry."

The lad let him enter the house. He led him through the dark passage—on the left was the door of Maria's room, to the right rose the staircase—into the yard, and quieted the dogs. He let Tarabas sit down on a pile of wood, and said that he would be back presently.

But he did not come. In his stead there came an old

man with a white beard. "Kabla! Turkas!" he called to the dogs. They ran to him.

It was old Andrey. Tarabas had recognized him instantly. Andrey had changed very much. He sniffed and peered about him cautiously as he went with his head bent forward and dragging feet. At first he seemed not to see Tarabas, but came on, followed by the dogs, with his head poked forward as though searching. His eyes then fell on Tarabas, seated on the wood-pile.

"Be very quiet," said old Andrey, "or the master might come. Wait; I won't be a minute."

He shuffled away and returned a few moments later with a steaming earthenware bowl and a wooden spoon.

"Eat, my boy, eat it up," he said. "Don't be afraid! The master's asleep—he lies down for half an hour every afternoon, so you've plenty of time. But when he gets up, he might come out here, and find you—that would never do. He used to be quite different, though."

Tarabas did not wait to be asked twice to eat. When he had finished, he still scraped the walls and bottom of the earthenware bowl for the last remains.

"Ssh! Ssh! Not so loud," said Andrey. "The old master might hear. I'm responsible, you see, for everything," he went on. "For forty years and more I've been in this house. I knew the old mistress, our master's mother, and his son, too. I saw both our chil-

dren come into the world, as you might say. And then
I saw the old mistress die."

"What has become of the son?" asked Tarabas.

"Well, he got into trouble first, and went off to
America. And then he was in the war. They waited
and waited for him after that. But he disappeared—no
one knows where. Not long ago—autumn last year it
was—the post-man brought a letter, though. It was a
yellow envelope with seals on it. It was just at dinner-
time. I still used to wait at table then, but now young
Yury does it—the lad that opened the door to you. I
see the master take the letter, and then he signs a
paper, and he gives it back to the post-man—I had to
go and get him his glasses out of the study. Then the
master reads the letter—not out loud, just to himself.
And then he takes off his glasses and he says: 'There's
no hope any more,' he said to the mistress. 'This letter's
from General Lakubeit, and that's what he says.' And
he gives her the letter. And she gets up and throws
down her knife and fork, and she screams out, just as
though I wasn't in the room—but she's forgotten me.
'No hope! You tell me that!' she shouts—at the master,
mind you. 'You dare to tell me that! You fiend—you
unnatural fiend!' And then she rushed away, out of the
room. You can imagine our surprise, for it was the first
time we had ever heard her raise her voice. She'd always looked as if she'd been crying, and so she did
always cry a lot, but never a word from her. And now,

all of a sudden, she's the one to make all that noise. Well, so she goes away from the table, but when she gets to the door she falls down. We had her ill for six weeks after that. Then she got well enough to get up again, but by that time the master was ill too—he'd never said a word about the letter or anything, but he must have grieved over it; in silence, you know. We had to push him about in a wheel-chair for a few weeks, but now he can get about on two sticks."

"And you—what do you think about it all?" asked Tarabas.

"Me? It's not my place to think. It's God's will, whatever comes. They say, the master has made a will giving all his fortune to the church. The notary was here, and the priest as well. What do you think of such a thing! A great fortune like his, to the church! But they say, it's done already, and they're nothing more than tenants in their own house. The master drives to town once a month, and once it was Yury that went with him. He said he'd seen him pay the rent at the post-office. But he can still drive himself— he can manage the reins quite well. And if you saw him up on the driver's box, you'd think nothing ailed him."

"I want to go somewhere, Father," said Nicholas. "I've come a long way. Can you show me where?"

The old man pointed towards the hall of the house.

A mad and irresistible plan was taking shape in Tara-

bas's mind. He would carry it out without delay. He
raced upstairs, four steps at a time. He opened the
door of his room. It lay in a bleak brown twilight; the
shutters were fastened over the window. Nothing had
been changed. The closet was still against the right-
hand wall, the bed was still on the left. But it was
stripped of covers, the red-and-white striped mattress
lay bare upon the springs. It looked like the skeleton
of a bed, hideously skinned. An old green overcoat—
Tarabas had worn it as a boy—hung on a nail behind
the door. At the foot of the bed stood a pair of shoes.

Tarabas picked these up, and put them in his pockets,
one right and one left. He shut the door behind him,
listened, and once again, as he had so often done before,
slid down the banister on his hands. He opened the
dining-room door. His father was in an arm-chair by
the window, asleep. Tarabas stood on the threshold and
looked at him. If anyone should find him there, he
could say he had made a mistake in the door. He stood
a while watching his father's cheeks puff in and out,
and the moustache rise and fall with them, and Tarabas's heart was quite cold. His father's hands lay inert
on either arm of the chair; wasted hands along the
backs of which the thick veins stood out, powerful
blood-streams, swollen yet congealed, underneath the
thin coating of the skin. There had been a time when
Tarabas had kissed those hands; they were brown and
muscular then, they smelt of tobacco and stables, earth

and weather, and were not merely hands, but also
more, the symbols of royal-parental power, a special
kind of hand, unlike all others, which only a father,
his father, might possess.

The window was wide open. The scent of the sweet
May rain was in the room, and the perfume of the
chestnut-candles, late in blooming. The father's lips,
invisible behind the thick moustache, opened and closed
with every breath he drew, emitting loud noises that
were strange and funny, yes, ribald. They seemed to
mock the dignity of sleep and sleeper, and came between the son and the reverence to which he would
gladly have given himself up in unseen contemplation
of his father. He longed for the cold awe, even for the
fear, with which his father had inspired him in the
olden days. But he found his feeling rather one of pity
for the faint absurdity of this old man asleep, so helplessly, so utterly surrendered to the organs of his body
as they struggled weakly, whistling, for air; and far,
far from lying there a mighty king wrapped in repose,
he looked rather like a comical victim of sleep and
broken health.

And yet for a moment the son felt that he was in
duty bound to kiss his father's lifeless hand. Yes, for a
moment it seemed to him that he had come there for
that purpose only. The feeling grew so strong that he
no longer thought of what danger might threaten him
if anyone were suddenly to open the door and find him

there. He moved very quietly over to the arm-chair, knelt down cautiously, and breathed a kiss over the back of his father's nearest hand. Then he turned away immediately, and reached the door again in three silent strides. Noiselessly he pressed the latch and opened the door, and went out of the house through the hall, as he had come. He returned to the yard and sat down again beside Andrey.

"Well, you were long enough in that elegant place," the old man jested. "We've only had those new-fangled ones about a year. That's the English style of water-closets, and we had them put in because there was no making the others decent again after we'd had the soldiers billeted on us time after time."

"Yes, they're very fine closets," said Tarabas. "Pity there'll be no one to inherit them."

"Oh, well—our young lady will go on living here. If she ever does marry, there'll be something put aside for her dowry, so they say. But it isn't likely that she'll find anyone now. The men have all been wiped out—those that might have done. There's none of them left, far and wide. And then, of course, she's not pretty, our young lady, poor thing. She looks just like her mother even now, young as she is. Sickly and thin, and as if she's always crying. Now her cousin Maria, she wasn't like that. She's in Germany now. Went off with one of those Germans, she did. They say he married her, but I've my doubts about it. She was engaged to our young master, too—there was plenty of talk about that. They say he was in too much of a hurry to wait for the wedding—you know. And 'once fell, never well,' as the saying goes. They say, she had no fault to find with the war—well, the German gentleman must have noticed that too. . . ."

"All sorts of things go on among the rich folk," said Tarabas.

"There's no rich at all any more," Andrey gossiped on. "Poor things! Everywhere else in Russia except here, they've had everything taken away from them, and shared out among the poor. God save me from such things, I say! I know my own luck, that I'm here, not there. . . . Look, there goes the mistress—see, over yonder."

She was wearing a long, black dress and a black lace cap. Her trembling head drooped down so low that Tarabas could catch no more than a fleeting glimpse of waxen skin, shimmering yellowly, and the pointed profile of her nose. She crossed the yard with little, irregular steps. A swarm of cackling hens greeted her with noise and flapping of wings.

"She feeds the chickens, poor soul!" said Andrey.

Tarabas watched her. He heard how his mother, imitating the voices of the fowl, sent forth clucking, crowing, cheeping, quacking sounds. Greyish-yellow wisps of hair escaped from underneath her cap and fell about her face. His mother herself became, in that set-

ting, something like a clucking hen. The whole picture of her there was foolish in the extreme; he saw her
as an aged, black-clad simpleton, and it was clear beyond a doubt that the stupid fowl surrounding her had
been for many years her only companions.

And Tarabas watched her, saying to himself: "Her
womb bore me, she nursed me at her breasts, her voice
sang me to sleep. That is my mother."

He got up, went to her, stepping into the midst of the
fowl, bent very low, and murmured: "Lady!"

Her pointed chin came up; her little red-rimmed
eyes, with a few wisps of whitish-yellow hair blowing
over them, cast not a look at Tarabas. She turned round
and screamed: "Andrey! Andrey!" in a croaking voice.

At the same moment a window opened in the upper
story of the house. Old Tarabas's head appeared. He
shouted:

"Andrey! Where is that good-for-nothing? Throw
the tramp out! Go through his pockets! Where's Yury?
How many times have I got to tell the lot of you that
I won't have beggars in my place! To hell with you
all!"—The old man's voice capsized; he leaned still
farther over the window-sill, the blood rushed to his
head, and he screeched: "Get rid of him! At once! At
once!" countless times without stopping.

Andrey took Tarabas gently by the arm and led him
to the back gate.

"Go with God!" said Andrey softly. Then shut the

heavy gate with much noise. It creaked on its hinges and fell to with a heavy crash of irretrievable finality. It quivered a little with the force of it.

Tarabas took the willow-path, the narrow way between the marshes.

26

A FINE, dry summer set in. But it did not warm the heart of Tarabas. The torn boots in which he had gone home for the last time he had thrown away in the swamps behind the house. They were lost to sight in a moment. There was first a slight gurgling, then the green face of the marsh had smoothed itself out again without a wrinkle to show where they had sunk. Before leaving the narrow path beside the willow trees, Tarabas put on the other shoes that he had brought with him. Trusty and faithful shoes, they had waited for him all the years of the war, and since, at the foot of his own bed. He had worn them in America. In those shoes—they pinched a little now—he had roamed the stone streets of New York every evening on his way to fetch Katharina from her work. This must be the very spot, too, where he had met Maria years ago. He remembered the rage of passion with which he had stared at the lacings of her boots; and how the two of them had trod the narrow way, one behind the other with such care, lest they miss the path and step into the marsh; and the turmoil of their senses as they pressed on impatiently towards the wood.

Those were the events of a long by-gone life. Remembrance of them lay within Tarabas, dead and cold, corpses of memories. Like a stone coffin his heart enclosed them. The sky of home, the meadows of his childhood, the familiar song of the frogs, the sweet, mild soughing of the rain, even the perfume of the limes in early blossom, and the well-known monotonous knocking of the wood-pecker, all were dead to Tarabas, although they were all round him, and he could feel and hear them. It was as though, in the moment when he had kissed his sleeping father's hand, he had taken leave not only of the house in which he was born, and of his birthright and his home, but also of every sentiment for them and for the past. So long as he had still feared to set his foot over the threshold of the house again his parents and his sister and the landscape of home had been alive; living objects of that dangerous nostalgia which might yet have the power to seduce Tarabas from his endless, aimless wanderings. How foolish the fear had been! An unknown, mustachioed, crippled man was his father; a frightened, grey-haired simpleton, his mother. If love had lived in either of them years ago, now they were cold and empty, like Nicholas himself. He might have said: "I am your son," and they would not have had the power to open their hearts to take him in, for their hearts were no longer alive, but had turned to stone. Had they died, had he come home to find only their two graves, his

warm remembrance could have brought them back to
life again, them and the house. But they were not dead;
they moved about, or stood; they slept and fed the
chickens; they chased beggars from their door—they
were animated mummies, in which they themselves
were buried, each one his own walking sarcophagus.

As Tarabas came out of the little wood that ended
at the avenue of birches, he turned round once again.
He saw the shimmering white façade of the house
which closed the avenue at the far end, and the dark
silver of the trees in front of it. Between the house and
Tarabas the rain hung a flowing, thick grey curtain.

"It was all over long ago!" said Tarabas to himself.

Even in the hot noons of those summer days the
shivering frosts assailed him now more and more often.
His great body, which had not yet lost the strength
that dwelt in it, was borne down by the fierce fever,
which accompanied him throughout the halcyon summer days like his own personal and separate winter.
Without warning, just as its inexplicable moods would
prompt, it leapt upon him. And Tarabas learnt not to
resist its onslaughts any more, as one learns in time not
to resist the shadow that each man has inseparably
attached to him. Sometimes he lay exhausted on the
edge of the road, and felt the good sun and the radiant
sky as through a thick, cold wall of glass, and froze
and shivered. There he would lie, and wait for the
pains to come, in the back and in the chest, together

with the fits of helpless coughing. These took place
with a certain regularity; one could await them confi-
dently, like faithful, dependable enemies. Sometimes
blood would flow from his mouth. It reddened the rich
green of the slope, or the light, earthy grey of the road.
Tarabas had seen the flowing of much blood in his
time, had caused much to flow. He spat it from him,
red liquid life. It dropped out of him and away. Sometimes, when he felt that the great weakness was coming on him, he would go into a tavern, fumble a coin
or two out of his bag, and drink a glass of strong spirits.
This was followed by hunger, as in his old days. It was
as though his body still remembered the old Tarabas
whom it had once enclosed within itself. The stomach
still felt hunger, the throat thirst. The feet still desired
to walk, and then to rest. The hands still desired to
grasp and touch things. And when the night came, the
eyes closed and sleep descended upon Tarabas. And
when the morning broke, it was as though Tarabas had
to wake himself by force, and scold his limbs for being
tired and lazy; he had to order his feet to move, command them to march, as he had once commanded his
regiment to do these things.

Regularly on every fifteenth day of the month, he
appeared in the great hall of the post-office in the capital. And regularly he was met by the young man, who
handed him his pension. These meetings were at-
tended by a certain laconic ceremonial. Tarabas raised

two fingers to his cap, while the young man lifted his hat respectfully. He said: "Thank you very much, sir!" when Tarabas had signed. He raised his hat again when they separated.

One day, however, he did not go at once but stood a while regarding Tarabas, and said then: "If I may take the liberty of suggesting it, sir, I think you should see a doctor. Hadn't I perhaps better say something to His Excellency?"

"Say nothing whatever, please!" said Tarabas.

He inspected his face in the little mirror of the weighing-machine which had been lately set up in the vestibule of the post-office, in order to give it the final touch of modernity. And he saw that his eyes were sunk deep in their sockets, and that a thick network of tiny blue veins criss-crossed both his temples. He stood on the platform and dropped a coin into the slot. He weighed one hundred and eight pounds just as he was.

He went out smiling, like one who has at last learnt what he is to do. He left the capital by the road along which the dairy-farmer had driven him a few months before. A mile down, there was a parting of the ways. At this point there stood two ancient, weather-faded wooden sign-posts with arrows. On the left-hand one could be deciphered the half-erased word, "Koryla." The arrow on the other pointed to the right towards Koropta. Tarabas took the road to Koropta.

He went slowly, almost meditatively. He did not want to reach the little town before nightfall. He seemed to be sunk in long-drawn sweet anticipation of an inescapable happiness that must await him in Koropta. When the first cottages of the little town came into sight—it was late in the afternoon—his heart began to beat fast with joy. One more curve in the road, and already the wall round the inn of the White Eagle was within view. Tarabas granted himself a rest. For the first time in many a long, long day the summer peace which lay upon the world entered him too. No fever had him in its grip. In the evening glory a happy swarm of tiny mayflies, golden in the sun, danced before his face. He watched their intricate play. He received it like a kind of welcome and recognition. The sun moved farther down the sky, the mayflies withdrew. Tarabas got up. When he reached Kristianpoller's inn it was already evening. Fedya was standing on a ladder outside the great brown door, pouring fresh oil into the red lantern which hung on an iron arm at right-angles to the wall.

"Praise be to Jesus Christ," cried Tarabas to Fedya above his head.

"World without end, amen, I'm coming!" answered Fedya busily. He clambered down, can in hand, and said: "Come inside!"

Tarabas sat down in the yard on one of the barrels. He saw the out-house in front of him. Its walls had

been newly white-washed, and the old door replaced
by a new one painted black. Fedya brought meat, potatoes, and beer, and Tarabas, pointing to the out-
house said:

"What is that over there?"

"It's a chapel now," said Fedya. "Nobody knew it
for a long time. But one day the picture of the Madonna
suddenly came out on the wall—all by itself, just think
of that! It was a miracle. She got down from the wall
and stretched out her arms and blessed the soldiers in
their sleep—but they woke up and saw her. And then
everyone went out into the streets and began to beat
the Jews, but the priests came, and preached to the
people. They said the Jews were not to blame. My own
master, the inn-keeper here, he's a Jew. And I know
he's innocent as the first snow. He's even had a chapel
made of the place—it used to be his lumber-room. On
Sundays the priests say mass here. It's good business for
us, I can tell you, because the peasants can hardly wait
till mass is over before they make a bee-line for the
bar. We have our hands full on Sundays. We make
even more on Sundays than on pig-market day."

Meanwhile Tarabas ate his plate clean, thoroughly,
without haste and serene in spirit. It grew dark; Kristianpoller in the parlour was lighting the big round
lamp.

"I must go now," said Fedya, and took Tarabas's

empty plate. He wanted to say: "And so must you!"
But he waited a while yet.

"Have you still far to go?" he asked.

"No," said Tarabas. "I'm almost home now."

He got up, thanked Fedya, and went down the high
street of Koropta. On either side they had begun to
rebuild the houses that the fire had burnt and dev-
astated. In front of the half-finished buildings the
women sat and gossiped as before. Girls were driving
a new generation of hens and ducks and geese home
for their night's rest; they urged them forward with
waving arms and billowing skirts. Infants mewed.
Children cried. Jews were returning, black and hurrying, from the occupations of the day. They had begun
to shut their garish little shops. Iron bars clattered. The
first stars glittered in the sky.

Tarabas's way was straight ahead. At the end of the
high street a by-path turned into a field. It led to the
Jews' cemetery. The little grey wall shimmered through
the blue of the summer night. The gate was locked. In
the cottage where the caretaker lived light was still
burning. Tarabas vaulted the wall without a sound. For
a while he groped up and down among the hundreds
of gravestones, all alike in rows; he lit a match each
time to light the angular characters which he could
not read, and paused to look at the strange drawings—
two hands outspread in benediction with the thumbs

joined at their tips, a lion with eagle's wings upon its back, a six-pointed star, two open pages of a book covered with the indecipherable writing.

In front of the last row of graves—a small space still waited for the next dead Jews—Tarabas scooped out a little hole in the earth with his hands, undid one of the two bags from round his neck, laid it in the hole, filled up the hole with earth again, and smoothed it with his hands. An owl cried somewhere, a bat flew by, the sky of night streamed forth its deep and luminous blue and the brilliance of its stars.

"It was a red beard," said Tarabas to himself. "It frightened me. I have buried it."

He left the cemetery by the way he had entered it, over the wall, and turned back along the by-path. It was quite quiet in the little town. Only the dogs, hearing Tarabas go by, began to bark. He found a shelter for the night in one of the cottages which had only just begun to be rebuilt. It smelt of damp mortar and fresh lime. Tarabas slept the night in a corner, awoke with the sunrise, and went out into the street. He met the earliest of the pious Jews, hurrying to the synagogue, stopped them, and asked where Shemariah lived. They were astonished at his question, gave no answer, but stood and looked at him a long while.

"You needn't be afraid of me," said Tarabas—and it seemed to him that someone laughed, as he spoke these words. Was anybody still afraid of him? It was the first

time in his life that he had said such a thing. Would
it have ever occurred to him to say it while he was still
the mighty Tarabas—could he have done so then?
"We've known each other for a long time, Shemariah
and I," he went on.

The Jews exchanged inquiring, knowing glances,
then one of them said: "If it's Shemariah you want,
you'd better ask at Nissen's. The blue shop, three doors
from the market-place."

The shop-keeper Nissen was sitting beside a samovar
in which maize was cooking. His many-coloured wares
were spread out all around him, and he was on the
look-out for customers. He was a comfortable, elderly
man with a grey beard and the portliness that denotes
the man of substance. An esteemed citizen of Koropta
and a passionate philanthropist, he seemed already to
have received the safe assurance that his benefactions on
earth had caused a place to be reserved for him in the
Jews' heaven, ready for him to enter when the time
came.

"Yes," he said. "Shemariah lives here with me, in the
attic. The poor simple creature! You used to know him
in the old days, did you? Do you know his story? Well,
there was a colonel here—a new one; Tarabas was his
name—may it be wiped out! But they say he died of
a stroke soon after—what a merciful death for such a
villain! Well, this colonel—he pulled out poor Shemariah's beard. Just as he was on his way to bury a

Torah. Ever since then he's been quite foolish. He
couldn't work any more, or anything. So I said to myself: 'You take him in, Nissen!' What can you do?
Someone has to look after these poor souls. He lives
with me, like my brother. You can go upstairs to him
if you like."

It was a tiny attic which housed Shemariah, with a
round sky-light instead of a window. A wooden bench
was spread with Shemariah's bed-clothes; this bench
was what he slept on. As Tarabas entered, he was sitting at the bare table with a large book open in front
of him; he was humming to himself as he read. He
must have thought that it was someone he knew who
had come into the room, for it was some time before he
raised his head. But then a shock of terror transformed
his face. His terror blazed, an icy fire, in his staring
eyes. His humming song broke off; he gazed at Tarabas in a paralysis of fear. His lips moved, but no sound
came from them.

"I am a beggar," said Tarabas. "Don't be afraid,
Shemariah." Then he added: "Have you a piece of
bread to spare for me?"

It was a long time before the Jew Shemariah could
grasp the words. The language he could hardly understand; he must have realized Tarabas's wish simply by
the ragged clothes he wore, his attitude, his gestures.
He uttered a shrill titter, rose, clung fearfully to the
wall, and slunk along it, with one shoulder half turned

to the stranger, still tittering, to the bed. From underneath the pillow he pulled out a piece of dry bread,
laid it on the table, and pointed to it with his finger.
Tarabas approached the table, Shemariah pressed himself against the bed. Tarabas saw that all round the
Jew's thin, freckled face a short and meagre, fan-like
beard of silver hair had grown, with bare scars between, as though it had been gnawed by mice. It was
a shabby garland of pitiful silver which had begun to
clothe the marred face again.

Tarabas's eyes fell; he took the bread and said: "I
thank you." He left the room. On the way down the
narrow ladder which led to the attic, he began to eat
the bread. It tasted of Shemariah's sweat and bed.

"He didn't recognize me," said Tarabas to the shop-
keeper Nissen, when he came downstairs again. "God
be with you!"

"Here's a maize-cob just done," said Nissen. "Take it
with you to eat on the way!" One should do good to all
the poor, said the shop-keeper to himself. But a poor
man may also be a thief; one need not let him remain
in one's shop longer than necessary.

"All in good order," Tarabas thought, and went his
way. "It is all in good order now."

27

A FEW weeks later—the summer was already nearing its end, the chestnuts were ripening and the Jews of Koropta were getting ready to celebrate their high festivals—there came to the general store kept by the shop-keeper Nissen the gentle Brother Eustachius from the Lobra monastery near by. The good brethren of Lobra occupied themselves with the care of the sick; some of the brethren were accomplished surgeons and physicians, and there were even Jews in Koropta who, when they fell ill, went neither to the local quacks nor to the doctors, but to the monks.

Sometimes, at certain seasons of the year, they would come—always only two—to the little town to make a collection for the poor. A strange feeling would then take possession of the Jews—compounded of the alien and the familiar, of gratitude, respect, and fear. While the little round caps worn by the monks upon their shorn skulls were things that they knew well, so much the greater was their terror of the great metal crucifixes which hung like a weapon upon each brother's hip, the cross which their forefathers were accused of having erected for an unspeakably dreadful purpose, which was a symbol to all the peoples of the earth that they would be blest, and to them only the token of suffering and damnation.

One of the monks had rid this Jew and that one of an aching tooth; another had applied the leech to others, or lanced an abscess. But only while they still endured their pains could the Jews feel close to their Samaritans; fear of the torment of sickness could banish for an hour or two the other, and far greater, fear— that which was born and bred in the blood. Yet in the days of health their gratitude to the godly brethren survived, and dwelt in them side by side with mistrust. As the brethren, unlike the lay healers, accepted no money for their services, one turned to them gladly, but when one was well again one asked oneself what reason these incomprehensible men could have for treating Jews for nothing. Now, it may be that the pious brethren knew, or at least divined, these sage reflections; at all events they combined with the commandment to waken their neighbours' charity by means of pious exhortation to almsgiving, also the good purpose of hiding their strange selflessness a little from the shrewd Jews, and this was shrewd on their part.

In the Jewish houses the almsgiving was a rapid, almost hasty, ceremony. Money, clothes, and food were brought to the monks outside the door, in order that they might not cross the threshold. Their billowing, coarse brown frocks, the ample roundness of their well-

fed bodies, their ruddy, shining faces, their unvarying
gentleness, their complete indifference to cold and heat,
rain, snow, and sun—these things all seemed unnatural
to the Jews, inclined as they were to worry endlessly
and always, yes, positively to wallow in their cares.
Each morning they began by fearing what the day
would bring; long before the winter came, they shivered in the frost to come, and in the summer they
wasted away to skeletons; for ever agitated because
they never did, and never could, feel that this land was
home to them, they had long since lost what they once
knew of calm, and lived their lives buffeted and tossed
hither and thither between hate and love, anger and
servility, protest, uprising, and pogrom.

For years they had been used to seeing the brethren
from the monastery of Lobra appear in the little town
at fixed seasons of the year. Now, however, when one
of them arrived at quite another season, they began to
dread the approach of some new disaster. What could
be his errand? Whither was he bound? They stood in
trembling suspense outside their shops, ready to plunge
into hiding at a moment's notice. Meantime the comfortable figure of the gentle monk Eustachius moved
deliberately and unsuspectingly past all the fears on
either side of him, down the miry middle of the street,
lifting the skirts of his robe a little, and striding serenely
in his thick high-boots with their double soles. Here
and there an over-zealous peasant woman sprang down

from the wooden sidewalk to kiss his hand. He was used to such things. With automatic dignity he put out his strong brown hand, let it be kissed, and wiped it on his robe. The anxious glances of the Jewish shop-keepers followed him. The watchers saw how he stopped at Nissen's, read the sign above the door, and mounted the high sidewalk with one huge step. He vanished into the shop.

The dealer Nissen rose, startled and apprehensive, from the stool on which he sat. Brother Eustachius smiled gently, produced out of the depths of his robe an ivory box, and offered the Jew a pinch of snuff. The Jew reached into the box, sneezed heartily, and asked: "Reverend Father, what do you want of me?"

"Don't be afraid," said the monk, "but my errand is a very sad one. We have a sick man in our monastery; it will be all over with him very soon. The foolish Shemariah lives with you, I know. That was a good work of yours, to take him in. Yes, I wish such good hearts as yours could be found in all Christians."

Somewhat calmed, but still mistrustful, Nissen an-swered with a general observation: "God commands us to be merciful."

"But God is seldom obeyed by men," replied Eu-stachius. "You took a burden on you of your own free will. It must be very difficult to get on with that Shemariah. Do you think that I could talk to him?"

"Reverend Father—it is impossible!" said the dealer

Nissen. And his eyes considered the robe, the rosary, the crucifix. The monk followed the look and understood.

"Very well," he said. "Will you go with me to him then? It is like this, you see. That sick man of ours says that he would like to die, but cannot. He says that he did this Shemariah great harm and wrong, and Shemariah must first forgive him. Do you know what the trouble was? Or what he means? It is possible," continued Eustachius—for he had decided to make a concession to that common sense which rules the minds of Jews, "there is of course a possibility that he is only imagining it, for he is in a high fever, and he may be raving in delirium. But one must do what one can, so that he may die in peace. You understand?"

"Very well," said Nissen. "I will go with you."

And the dealer Nissen, not without trepidation, conducted the monk up the narrow ladder to Shemariah's attic room. When they had reached the door, he said: "I had better go in first, Reverend Father." He entered, but left the door open.

Shemariah glanced up from the great book which he seemed to pore over eternally. Behind his host and friend, Nissen, he became aware of the terrifying, fat, and alien figure of the brown-frocked monk. He shut the book sharply, got up, and went over to the wall, pressing close against it for protection. As he stood, with his emaciated head framed in the round sky-light, which was the only window in the room, he reminded the gentle Brother Eustachius of a saint or one of the apostles. Shemariah's two thin hands, jutting far out of the sleeves of his caftan, were outstretched against his guests. His lips quivered. But he said nothing.

"Shemariah, listen carefully now to what I tell you," Nissen began, going to the table. "You need not be afraid. The gentleman hasn't come to take you away and lock you up. He has only come to ask you if you will do something for him—he has a little favour to ask of you. Come, say 'yes.'—Then we'll go away again at once."

"What does he want?" Shemariah asked.

"There's a man lying ill in his house—very ill. He's going to die." Nissen made a movement of the head to indicate the monk, who still stood at the threshold and had not come into the room. "This sick man says that he once did something terrible to you, and he can't die in peace because of it. You must say that you are not angry with him, only that. Just 'yes'—that's all you need to say."

It was a long time before Shemariah moved. Then he left the place against the wall where he had taken refuge. And to Nissen's astonishment he said in a loud voice:

"I know who he is. Let him die in peace; I'm not angry with him."

And to the dealer's blank amazement, Shemariah came round the table close up to him, raised his right hand, putting the nail of the thumb against the nail of the first finger, and said:

"I've nothing against him, tell him, not this much! He shall die in peace. Tell him so!"

28

IN Brother Eustachius's cell, and in his bed, lay Nicholas Tarabas. He was waiting. On the stone floor beside the bed a fire was burning, so that the sick man might have the warmth he needed. One of the brethren sat by him at the other side of the bed.

Eustachius entered, and Tarabas sat upright in the bed.

"He has forgiven," said Eustachius.

"Did you speak to him yourself?"

"I did," answered Eustachius.

"How is he then? Can he still be sensible? Does he know what he is saying?"

"He's very sensible indeed," said Eustachius. "He understood it all, perfectly. He's a great deal clearer than they think."

"Is he? Well ... And his son?"

"He said nothing about his son."

"Pity!" said Tarabas, and lay back on the pillows.

"I should like," he said then, "to be buried in Koropta. Please let someone send word to my father and mother and sister; and General Lakubeit must also be told."

Those were Tarabas's last words. He died that evening as the sun was going down. Through the cell's iron window-bars it cast eight burnished squares upon the coverlet, over which a gentle quiver passed, in the last second.

They buried Colonel Nicholas Tarabas in Koropta with all the military honours due to his rank. There was music, and a volley was fired over the grave. The Jews of Koropta were at the cemetery too. Accompanying the father, who hobbled to the graveside on his two handsome ebony sticks, the veiled mother and the old servant Andrey had come.

After the funeral the parents entered the black carriage, and Andrey drove them away. None of those present had seen a tear in the eyes of old Tarabas.

On the road the carriage overtook the troop returning to the barracks to the bright music of the brass.

Brother Eustachius ordered a head-stone for the dead man, a beautiful stone of black marble. Eustachius knew no more about him than the dates of his birth and death. Had it been possible, he would have had the stone inscribed with the words: "A fool that deserved to enter heaven." But this could not be called suitable as an epitaph. Therefore Brother Eustachius meditated over the matter of a suitable one.

29

A WEEK later he went with the notary to the Jew Nissen. They climbed, all three, the ladder up to Shemariah's attic. Shemariah rose from his seat, and shut the book.

He no longer fled before the sight of strangers. He merely rose, and remained standing by the table, with his closed book in front of him.

In the presence of the two witnesses, the reverend Brother Eustachius and Nissen Pichenik, general dealer, he declared Shemariah Korpus, sexton, sole heir of Colonel Nicholas Tarabas, recently deceased. The legacy consisted of a bag of gold coins to the value of five hundred and twenty gold francs, and a few hundred bank-notes.

The notary put the money down on the table. Brother Eustachius and the dealer Nissen counted the gold pieces, and the notary shovelled them back into the bag. The bag was then handed to Shemariah across the table.

He balanced it in his right hand, tittered, transferred it to his left. He held it by the string, flicked at it with one finger of his right hand and set it spinning with a clinking sound. He gazed at it a while with an expression of happiness, and finally let it fall upon the table.

"I don't need it," said Shemariah at last. "Take it away. You can have it."

As, however, nobody moved to take it, he began without another word to offer them the little bag one after the other, first the notary, then the dealer Nissen, and lastly the monk Eustachius. But each one pushed it back.

Shemariah waited a while. Then he took the bag, went over to his bed, and put it underneath the pillow.

The three men left him. On the way down the ladder the notary said: "All that good money wasted—too bad! So he lived in vain after all, that Tarabas!"

"That we don't know," said Brother Eustachius. "That is something we can never know."

They took their leave of the dealer Nissen.

"Let's go over to Kristianpoller's for a moment," the notary proposed.

A few moments later they were sitting in Kristianpoller's parlour. The one-eyed inn-keeper came to their table. "Well, he's dead now," he said.

"He was one of your guests," remarked the notary.

"For a long time," the Jew Kristianpoller answered. "He was a queer guest in the Kristianpoller inn."

"I should say," said the notary, "that he was a queer guest on earth altogether."

This struck the ear of the monk Eustachius. And he decided to have Tarabas's gravestone inscribed with this inscription:

COLONEL NICHOLAS TARABAS
A GUEST ON EARTH

It seemed to him a modest, just, appropriate epitaph.

30

AT the moment when these lines are being written, some fifteen years have passed since the death of the strange man whose story they have told. Over the grave of Colonel Nicholas Tarabas stands a simple cross of black marble, paid for by old father Tarabas.

The stranger visiting Koropta today can find no trace of these remarkable, sad, and wonderful events. All the houses in the little town have been renovated within and painted white without, and a building committee, modelled according to the western-European pattern, takes care that they are all put in order at the same time, and that they resemble each other to the last detail, like soldiers.

The old priest died a year or two ago. The foolish Shemariah still lives in the dealer Nissen's attic; he keeps the useless bag of gold underneath his pillow and can hardly be induced to touch it, let alone show it or give it out of his hand. As the new government of the country has its own coinage now, the old gold franc and ruble pieces have—as the dealer Nissen correctly observes—lost much of their original value. The attempt to convey this fact to Shemariah proved com-

pletely fruitless. He only tittered. It may be that the
fool was indeed laughing at the wise ones for their
wisdom. Perhaps it was clear to him alone that the
value of these gold coins never had been, nor could be,
a value of the kind that is noted on the quotation lists
of the world's banks and exchanges. Doubtless the
dealer Nissen nourishes an unspoken hope that he will
one day inherit the bag of money. It would be, at that,
no more than the obvious reward for his benefactions
to the foolish Shemariah. Moreover, other poor and
needy ones would have their share of it, if it fell to
him. For the dealer Nissen will be a man diligent in
charity and good works until he dies. He owes it to
God, to his reputation, and to his business also. And
probably the dealer Nissen is right.

In all Koropta he and the inn-keeper Kristianpoller
are the only ones who sometimes, over a glass of mead
—and the dish of salted dried peas which goes with it
—talk of the strange Colonel Tarabas, and how he
came, a mighty king, into the little town, to be buried
there a beggar. In Kristianpoller's out-house there still
stands an altar before the miraculous picture of the
Virgin, but services are held there less and less often
as time goes on. A new generation is growing up
which knows nothing of the old story. As in all the
years before it happened, the people go to the church
to pray. And the new generation is little given to praying at the best of times.

The pig-market comes round often. The little horses neigh, the pigs squeal, the peasants get very drunk. When they have reached the stage of helplessness, the servant Fedya takes their arms and drags them to their carts, where he sobers them with a flood of cold water. The Jews continue to deal in beads and kerchiefs, pocket-knives, scythes, and sickles. Every year hop-merchants from other parts come to Koropta. Many a one, taking a look round the neat little town, strolls down the high street, climbs the hill with the church on its summit, wanders through the grave-yard, and notices the odd epitaph:

Colonel Nicholas Tarabas
a guest on earth

The stranger returns to Kristianpoller's inn, drinks a beer, a mead, or a glass of wine, and says to the inn-keeper: "And by the way, I came across a very curious grave up there in that churchyard of yours!"

Nathan Kristianpoller—he himself knows not why—likes these guests best of all who come into his house. He sits down at the stranger's table and tells him the story of Tarabas.

"And you Jews are not afraid now, any more?" the stranger will sometimes ask.

"You know how it is"—Kristianpoller's answer is always the same—"people forget. They forget fear and they forget the terrors that they go through. They want to live at all costs; they make themselves get used to everything, because they want to live! It is quite simple. Even miracles, even the most extraordinary things— they forget them, too, quicker even than the everyday ones. For the everyday is what they want. See it yourself, sir—at the end of every life stands death. We all know it. And who remembers it?"

Thus speaks the inn-keeper Nathan Kristianpoller to the guests that he likes best.

He is a clever man.